# THE STOREKEEPER OF SLEEMAN

Jody, the young son of the Blacks who ran the general store in Sleeman, saw and heard most things that went on. He knew but avoided the wild men from the Arrowhead, its owner Piggott, the vicious foreman Spanish Jack, and the hard, brawling riders who spread fear in the town. Arrowhead smashed those in its path — men were beaten, the Allott's barn was fired, but nobody dared offer any opposition. Yet both Jody and his father were drawn into the streets of blazing death.

*Books by Lee F. Gregson*
*in the Linford Western Library:*

**THE MAN OUT THERE**

# LEE F. GREGSON

# THE STOREKEEPER OF SLEEMAN

*Complete and Unabridged*

# LINFORD
*Leicester*

First published in Great Britain in 1991 by
Robert Hale Limited
London

First Linford Edition
published July 1993
by arrangement with
Robert Hale Limited
London

British Library CIP Data

Gregson, Lee F.
  The storekeeper of Sleeman.—Large print ed.—
Linford western library
  I. Title II. Series
823.914 [F]

ISBN 0–7089–7370–1

Published by
F. A. Thorpe (Publishing) Ltd.
Anstey, Leicestershire

Set by Words & Graphics Ltd.
Anstey, Leicestershire
Printed and bound in Great Britain by
T. J. Press (Padstow) Ltd., Padstow, Cornwall

This book is printed on acid-free paper

# 1

NEAR noon a heavy freight wagon drawn by a four-horse team turned into a narrow back street in the town of Sleeman and came to halt in the yard in back of the general store. Fechney, the driver, grey-bearded and sweating, climbed down stiffly and stood flapping his old hat against dusty clothing, waiting for somebody to answer his call. At this hour the town was lying quietly in the heat; even the fitful breeze was warm and there was, in the occasional movement of tumbleweeds, a kind of lethargy and an emptiness that was, however, an illusion; for Sleeman was a good-sized cowtown with commercial buildings, several saloons and two hotels. The four sturdy horses stood with big heads drooping. The wagon was hooped and covered and a loose

1

corner of its canvas was flapping dolorously. Fechney scratched at his old vest, waiting. He always looked forward to making a delivery to the general store in Sleeman or rather, he had done so ever since the present owners, the Blacks, had bought the place about twelve months back. They had turned out to be a vast improvement on the narrow-faced, humourless Gilbey who had run it before that, a man of uncertain temper who had been somewhat slow to pay, as well.

It was the woman, Fran Black, who came out, small, with a good figure and with slightly faded good looks, and sometimes a sad air about her. Nonetheless, she greeted the old man warmly.

"You're early, Ned. You've made a good run."

"Passable. Passable, Miz Black. Got a heap o' stuff here fer Josh, an' I got them bolts o' cloth an' all."

"Oh, that's splendid. Josh will be along directly, but why don't you step in first for a bite and a cool drink to help lay the dust?"

Expecting the courtesy, he was already moving forward, removing his battered, greasy hat. "Right obliged, Miz Black. Right obliged." She sure was a good looking woman, he thought, her hair very dark, piled and pinned atop her head, her complexion pale but unflawed, her large eyes a deep blue. He followed her into the cool dimness of the kitchen as she called:

"Josh? Freight's here!"

★ ★ ★

The covered wagon with its pair of horses and a third animal on a lead, behind, was standing ready to move out from the overnight camp in the long, morning shadow of a rock pinnacle in rough, poor country that looked, nonetheless, as though it might get better up ahead.

The man and the woman had been at prayer and now rose to their feet,

3

brushing dust from their clothing. They were a young couple and seemed, by the appearance of their horses and wagon, to be well enough equipped for a journey across this rough land, yet the people themselves gave the impression of being out of their element. A tallish, skinny man, he was dressed in a sombre suit and black, medium-brimmed hat, no kind of wear for the heat that of a custom rose in intensity throughout the day, and his hands were more like the hands of an artist than of one who lived and worked in the cattle country. His wife, too, seemed a touch delicate, with a pale, though pretty face, brown hair worn in a large bun, and hazel eyes. She had on a dark blue dress and bonnet with a trim of white.

Their wagon was crammed with goods, furniture and chattels, boxes and baskets, and there were water casks slung on either side and a spare wagon wheel beneath. Clearly they were travelling with their worldly possessions, and the dusty state of the wagon and the heaviness about the eyes of its owners indicated that they had already covered some considerable distance.

He handed her up onto the seat and when she had flounced her skirt and settled herself, gave her the worn, leather-covered bible he had read from at their prayers, and she placed it alongside her. The angular young man then walked around and climbed up himself and unwound the long reins. Before them, the distance shimmered, and as far as they could see, no other living thing stirred.

"Sooner we start the sooner we get there," he remarked. "If it gets too hot for you, Emily, there's room, still, to sit back under the cover."

She nodded absently. Then:

"William, I just hope this really is the Sleeman trail."

"I feel sure it is," he said. "Anyway, in five, six hours at most, we'll know for certain." He flicked the reins and clicked his tongue and the heavy rig creaked into motion.

Rufe Stoll was the name of the Sleeman sheriff, big in stature, with more than a suggestion of a paunch, and an incipient roundness beneath the chin. He stood now at the window of his office looking out on Main, a tin mug of coffee in one hand. A man not given to overmuch talk, he tried to be aware of all that went on in the town, and took careful note of itinerant strangers. In particular he kept an eye on the riders from Arrowhead who came into Sleeman sometimes, and took special care if Seth Piggott, the man who owned the spread, was among them. Sheriff Stoll managed to tread a fine line with Arrowhead and he was brooding over it now, recalling trouble in one of the saloons only days ago, when he had had to step in to stop a fracas that had been rapidly turning ugly. Piggott himself had not been there, as it happened, but the Arrowhead ramrod, a dark, ravaged-looking man known only as Spanish

6

Jack, had, and for a moment, Stoll had thought him ready to challenge the authority of the law. Stoll was no fool. He would be seen to keep the peace, since that was where his wages came from, but he was ever mindful that he must step carefully sometimes, pick the moment to be seen in his official capacity, as well as the moment to be diplomatically busy elsewhere. Stoll was not lacking in sand, he had simply learned long ago as a lawman in other places like Sleeman, to weigh the odds and the consequences and see where the welfare of Rufe Stoll balanced with them.

Draining his coffee cup, he turned away and set it down on the littered desk. He had already looked through several reward dodgers that had come in recently, but among them there was no face of any interest to him. Presently, from a cupboard behind the desk, he fetched a bottle and a glass and poured a shot of whiskey. He was no great drinker and was not a public drinker at all, preferring to take a quiet glass now and again in privacy, savouring it, never going beyond two drinks at any one time. In various parts of the country, in his wandering youth, he had witnessed the deaths of three lawmen who, when it had really mattered, had been too fuddled to see what was coming. He strolled again to the window. At this particular hour there was not a lot of street activity but he took note of what there was, out of habit. A man from Arrowhead, with a buckboard with some lengths of lumber on it, was pulling away, heading out of Sleeman. This, he watched until there was only dust remaining, hanging in the air. On the opposite boardwalk, pacing along, loose-limbed, immaculately dressed, as was his custom, wearing a shallow, pearl-grey stetson, went a saloon-keeper. Ray LePage. A smooth one. Stoll thought. A smooth smart-ass, too educated by half for the likes of Sleeman. Smooth. Smooth face, smooth hands, smooth tongue. Always

8

Stoll looked at LePage with a mixture of mistrust and envy. LePage passed from his view. Two young boys went scuffing by in the street. One of them was Jody Black. Now there, thought Stoll, was another one that would bear watching, that boy's father, Josh Black, the owner, nowadays, of the general store, a man with a good looking but oddly sad little wife. Fran. The storekeeper troubled the Sleeman sheriff in a way that Stoll could not define; a tall, loose-limbed man, he ran his store most capably, caused trouble to no-one, indeed was inclined to be somewhat aloof from the body of townsfolk; and for some reason he did not seem to fit; and Stoll did not like people or pieces that did not fit.

★ ★ ★

White dust rose as four sweat-patched riders put their mounts down a shallow, shingly bank, and moved unhurriedly out across a grassy flat, headed towards a dark line of trees where a glittering

9

stream cut the range. Arrowhead, these riders were, but now off Arrowhead land, the rancher himself, Piggott, his foreman, Spanish Jack, and two others named Geffan and Leech. Nearer to the rich strand of trees along the water, Piggott held up one gloved hand and drew to a halt, all four horses blowing and screwing about. Piggott shoved his greasy hat back and, pointing, allowed his extended arm to swing slowly back and forth.

"All that stretch from the grey rock slide under the Shannon Hills there, along to Duane Canyon an' up to where we come down the bank back there, was all Crear's."

They sat hot saddles, studying narrow-eyed the broad sweep of country that their employer had indicated, and in examining it thus, saw too the huddle of the old Crear homestead and its outbuildings, a high barn among them, all beyond the trees on the opposite side of the stream.

"I don't see no beeves atall no

more," said Leech, "nor hosses nor nothin'."

"I told yuh," Piggott said, "he let it run down, Crear did, took to the coffin varnish, sold off stock, what varmints didn't run off. There's just the buildin's an' the land, now."

"An' the water," Spanish Jack said, flashing white teeth. "Sweet water."

Piggott grinned, nodding. "There's good grass here boys, an' plenty of it, an' it ain't nobody else's business no more." Broad, ox-like, Piggott looked to be outsized even on the big, deep-chested bay he rode, and his small black eyes were not eyes that were accustomed to showing pity, but were flat and dead, like the eyes of a fish. Spanish Jack was tall, not nearly as heavily-built, but a tough man, as he had to be as Piggott's ramrod, with a lined, pockmarked face. His dark brows and hair and his brown dog-eyes gave him a Spanish aspect, to be sure, and though he was not, had long ago accepted with a kind of sneering pride, the name that he had acquired somewhere down some trail long ago. But it was a brave man or a foolhardy one who thought to use the matter of this name as an insult. The other riders, Leech and Geffan, were rough men of the range who had ridden hard trails and now drew Piggott's wages and asked no questions. Leech wore a thick, drooping moustache, and Gefan, for reasons he had never gone into, a full beard. Hard men, too, these; like called to like, as Sheriff Stoll had thought, in appraising them.

It was Geffan who now asked: "Yuh reckon on some of us movin' in here, right off?"

Piggott shook his head. "Not yet; but soon. I jes' want you boys to know how the land lies, for when the time does come. An' that won't be long."

"Fair enough," Leech said.

Geffan scratched at his bushy beard. "Yuh sure there ain't nobody nowhere to claim it?"

Piggott shrugged. "He was a loner,

ol' man Crear. Nobody come near to this place, not for years." Nonetheless, he saw fit to add: "An' anyway, don't I recall somethin' about possession bein' several points o' the law?"

They laughed and wheeled their horses away.

★ ★ ★

Allie, in a white silk shift, sat in front of the mirror that was fixed above her cluttered dressing table, applying a powder puff to her forehead, dabbing and looking and dabbing again.

"Ray, I can't see properly in this light. Raise the shade, won't you?"

LePage paused in his search for a cuff-link, went across the room and did as she had asked. This room above LePage's Black Horse Saloon, now more clearly revealed, was well furnished, to a standard in fact not often encountered in towns such as Sleeman. It was a room which reflected the standards of the man who owned

13

the establishment, a man of some poise and education, again, an unlikely person to come upon in such a town, owning a saloon, and who now, having secured his cuffs, slipped easily into a grey, tailored coat, worn over a neat, figured waistcoat which was looped with a fine gold chain. The woman who now rose from her seat before the mirror was small, cream-skinned, with features that were regular and had not yet begun to coarsen. She was Allie Benbow, who could be as spit-mouthed as her employer and consort, LePage, was elegant and well-spoken. An ill-assorted couple, they had rubbed along together for seven years. Now she picked up a conversation they had begun earlier.

"You ought to get that fat Rufe Stoll to earn his keep, put a real strong hold on 'em before somebody gets his head shot off. And worse, gets it done here, in this place."

LePage adjusted a blue silk handkerchief in his top pocket. "All range men like to let off steam when they get their hands on some folding money. Arrowhead's certainly no different in that respect. It simply isn't possible to run a cowtown saloon like a mission, Allie, you must see that."

"You can try to run it a bit less like a war, or like an infirmary for the truly mad," she said. "One of the girls gets hurt, Ray, and I'll take a hand if you won't and if Stoll won't. It's not about to get better, that's my opinion."

"I'll have a word with Stoll," he said, "but I don't expect he'll do much. We shall simply have to calm things down in our own place, if needs be."

"Pah!" She was struggling into a gown with a too-tight bodice. "Here." She turned her back to him and he carefully hooked-and-eyed the garment all the way up.

"But we have to be careful. If anybody does have to intervene it must be me. I've already told everybody else to take no risk. Back off, mouths firmly closed, no reaction. I can't do more."

With a direct insight, Allie said:

"Arrowhead riders'll probably read that as weakness."

"They spend," he reminded her. "They always spend as though there's going to be no tomorrow."

"When they come in," she said sharply, "no tomorrow is what I worry about the most."

★ ★ ★

Jody Black was eleven years old, a sturdy, darkhaired boy, already with a flowing litheness about him that mirrored his father and the way his father moved. Right now, called in to supper, he had washed up and was passing his mother's critical inspection.

"M-m . . . well, not too bad. Supper's ready."

"Where's pa?"

"Coming, I hope." She raised her voice towards the shop. "Josh?"

A man's firm, deep voice called back: "One minute . . . "

Jody slid into his accustomed chair

while his mother busied herself at the stove, lifting warmed plates from a rack above it.

"There was a fight in The Black Horse again last night," said Jody.

"How do you know that? Jody, have you been hanging around that place?"

"No. Somebody told Aaron's pa. They say it was a rider from Arrowhead an' a drummer from Tucson."

"What drummer from Tucson?" The boy's father had come in from the now closed store up front, and was on his way to wash up for supper.

"At The Black Horse," Jody said. "There was a fight."

"Pay no attention to what goes on in The Black Horse or any of the other saloons," his father said. "It's all spurred by bad liquor; and liquor, good or bad, fires big talk. And those men who talk big finally have to back it." A tall, slim-hipped, powerful-looking man, he had dark good looks, but a face that had seen its share of wear and tear in the past. There was an old scar

17

above his left eyebrow and another low on the left cheek that could have been caused by a blade. He went on through to the small pump house out back. The woman's eyes had followed him but when, in a few minutes, he came back in and they all sat down to their supper, Black glanced at his son.

"I hope you weren't listening around that saloon, boy."

"No sir. Aaron's pa heard about it an' Aaron told me. It was a real bad fight an' the drummer, he got real beat, an' — "

"Jody." At that point his mother cut in. "What goes on over there isn't of any interest to us. You know our views on violence."

"Yes, ma-am."

For a moment the deep blue eyes of the woman found those of her husband. The increase in violent incidents in the town, many of them linked directly to the presence of riders from the Arrowhead ranch, an outfit that was showing a propensity for hiring some very hard men, had been in their minds more and more in recent weeks. It had in fact become something that weighed heavily on the mind of Fran Black in particular.

★ ★ ★

In the limpid light of evening, because they had come newly into town and because they now seemed uncertain of what to do next, Sheriff Stoll, thumbs hooked in his leather vest, walked unhurriedly across to their wagon.

"Evenin' folks. Name's Rufe Stoll, the law here in Sleeman."

"Good evening, sheriff. Our name is Allott; Emily and William Allott."

Casually, Stoll touched the wide brim of his hat to the pale, pretty woman.

"Where might yuh be headed? Or do yuh intend stayin' here in Sleeman?"

"We'll stay here just overnight," said Allott, "if we can find a hotel room and somewhere to put up the horses."

Stoll pointed to a long, double-storey

structure not far along the street.

"Besant's, along there is one of the two hotels here. Both clean. Nothin' to choose between 'em; an' there's a good livery just this side of it."

"That's surely a relief," the woman said, "for it's been a long, hot, tiring journey getting as far as Sleeman."

Stoll took note of their well-loaded wagon with the other horse tethered to it. "Might a man ask where yuh're headed?"

"We're trying to get to a place called Crear's," William Allott told him. "Dan Crear is my uncle — my mother's brother — and recently he wrote to us. He said he was ill and invited us both to come out here and settle with him on his property, as we are his only living relatives, and so that we might take over the place should he die. Do you know Dan Crear?"

Stoll was a touch taken aback but took good care not to show it to these people. Now that it had been said, he did indeed recall old Dan

Crear making one of his rare trips into Sleeman, to the stage depot, say, a couple of months back. No doubt about it, Crear had looked ill on the visit, shrunken and with yellowing skin. In fact, Fran Black, to whom Crear had spoken, had insisted that the elderly man rest at her house — the living quarters behind the general store — and take a good meal there before attempting to make the journey back to his own place. Well now, Stoll thought, this is something. At length he said:

"I'm sorry to say I got bad news for yuh, folks. Dan Crear's dead. He come into Sleeman an' he made it back out to his place, but Miz Black down at the general store was so plumb concerned at how he'd looked when he was in town, that she up an' took a buggy out there herself an' it was her that found him."

One of Emily Allott's pale hands stole to her cheek. William Allott's voice was low:

"Dead."

"Ain't pleased to be the bearer of bad news," said Stoll, outwardly calm; but his mind was restless now, recalling unsettling rumours that had found their way to him over recent days, that Piggott's Arrowhead, assuming there would be no legal claimants to the Crear Place, planned to ease some cattle down onto the flats, to the good grass flourishing there, and to the abundant water to be had. Claimants or not, the legalities of such a move, should it be made, had been troubling Stoll's mind, yet so had considerations of the more practical difficulties which might arise should he move to prevent Piggott from occupying the land. What he had learned during the past few minutes tended to relieve one problem but might well give rise to a new and even uglier one. Once Seth Piggott's will was set on doing something, Stoll could not bring to mind either people or events altering it. He took another appraising look at the young couple up on their wagon and was not impressed or encouraged by what he saw, in terms of durability. The young man had gone very quiet and the woman's head had sunk down. Stoll could have sworn she was praying. In view of his own silent assessment of them and their situation, Stoll thought wryly that if she was, that might not be too bad a thing.

# 2

THE liveryman was full of it of course, so that, after they had left Sleeman, word about the newly-arrived Allotts fanned out in all directions. Nobody had suspected that old Dan Crear had had kinfolks, or to be truthful, given the matter any thought.

"Come through here askin' fer ol' Dan, they did."

"Wa-al, they're a mite late, then."

"Who are they, to Dan?"

"Nephew, the young feller is. An' I'll tell yuh somethin' else, they're kinda quiet, earnest, religious folks. The woman said they don't own weepons of any sort."

Afterwards, the storekeeper, Black, said to his wife: "They'd not be budged on that at all. They've no hunting gun, even. Nothing."

"Then maybe that's a blessing. No-one can trump up excuses to do harm to them," Fran said. But there was no conviction in the way she said it.

"They're out of place here," he said, "they've come from a different world."

"There sure was a whole heap of stuff in that wagon," Jody said. "All sorts of stuff, an' they had a work horse hitched on behind. Looked like a real ol' dog, that one."

"They say they mean to work their land," said Black, "not be in cattle as old Crear once was, before he gave up and let it go to ruin."

"He was old and he was ill," she said. "Oh yes, he drank, too, near the end. There was plenty of evidence of it out on that place. I think he was trying to shut out the pain, poor old man."

"There was a bible, a real old one, on the wagon seat between 'em," Jody said. "One with a little lock on it."

His father nodded. "I saw it." And to Fran, he added: "They'll need all

25

the faith they can muster. I've heard it said quite openly that Arrowhead expected to get hold of the Crear spread for more grazing and good water. What they won't expect is this, and Seth Piggott won't like it one bit." Again their eyes met, over the head of the boy, and it seemed that the woman gave her husband an almost imperceptible shake of the head.

* * *

The boy, like most of his kind, was all eyes and ears. This town was a good piece smaller than the one they had come from but it was still filled with interest for him; and there were those days on which there was no school, when he ranged freely up and down the busy main street and through the narrow alleys and back ways, always watching and listening and learning all about Sleeman. Boys often enjoy this unquestioned passage, kicking their stones or cans along in apparent aimlessness, where grown men might be unwelcome; and so it was with Jody Black, walking alone or in the company of some friend from the Sleeman schoolhouse. Almost everybody in the town became accustomed to seeing the likeable boy. Sheriff Stoll knew him.

"Jody boy, mind how yuh go, there." Rufe Stoll had never managed to get much talk out of the father, and got only marginally more from the son; but there was a little, now and again, some of it tantalizing to be sure, to a naturally curious man.

"Oh, yeah, we was in Texas once. I don't remember much about Texas."

"Texas, huh?"

"Yeah, an' we was in Colorado, too. I remember Colorado better." And then, almost as though some secret voice within the boy had spoken to him, his bright intelligent eyes would cloud and he would say no more. Yet Stoll had an instinct that whatever the phantoms were that came near to the boy at such times, he had no distinct sight of them himself, but was more likely to be obeying some firm ordinance which had been imposed upon him at some time in the past: "Tell nothing, boy. It's nobody else's business where you've been. That was then. This is now."

Jody knew Childs, the blacksmith, physically strong, gleaming with sweat, clanging his bouncing hammer on glowing iron in the flush and the bluish haze of his forge. He knew Fechney too, the old freighter who came and went at regular intervals, who was the lifeline of the general store; and he waved and called to the more genial of the cowboys passing through the town. And there was one of the saloon-keepers whom he found to be a fascinating man, whose speech and tone and manner was definitely not that of the range, LePage of the grey suits and the pearl-grey hat and black string tie, slim black stogie between his shining teeth, standing on the boardwalk outside his place, The Black Horse Saloon, and who always spoke to him pleasantly if he passed by. And with the instinctive, secret and mysterious certainty of the young, Jody knew that Ray LePage, narrow-eyed and thoughtful, sometimes watched as the boy's father moved about in the general store which stood almost directly across on the opposite side of Main. The boy saw it and pondered over it and thought back. Now that he was older he could not rightly have said whether or not some of the things that were in his head and that came back sharply sometimes, had really happened. For the very young, some memories, some faces and voices, some days and nights, stay crisp and clear and well-remembered always; others seem to dwell in some kind of half-life, a twilight-time, some place whose borders are indistinct, whose memories cannot be trusted totally, because they will not come clear.

The men from the cattle lands had always held a fascination for the boy, too. Hard men they were, leather-clad and hung with leather and metal, thick shellbelts, heavy Colt pistols, gleaming steel spurs clanking as they paced the boardwalks, range men, dusty, spitting, loud, sweating when they came into Sleeman to spend up their pay. Forty-a-month-and-found. The saloon lamps would not have been lit two hours before the first of the fights began, and if the Bar Dog in that particular saloon could not manage to stop it, somebody would likely run to fetch Stoll, and if he considered it to be serious enough he would curse and slap his hat on and go stumping down there and make some curt peace-keeping talk, and then he would go away and would not return until maybe sent for again because they had begun seriously breaking the furniture. Wild, high-spirited boys they were, mostly, but there were some bad bastards too, rather more of that sort of late; plenty of drifters too, a different summer name, year-to-year and don't turn your back, some of them, a special, chilling look about them. Jody Black saw them all, looking and listening, kicking his stones, but like everybody else, he made sure that he kept his distance. And some men who lived closer to Sleeman than these dangerous itinerants, men like Piggott and Spanish Jack in particular, made you go real cold, somehow.

★ ★ ★

Spanish Jack, dusty and streaked with sweat, sat his saddle, looking down at Stoll.

"The hell yuh say! Who are they?"

"They're kin o' Dan Crear's. Wa-al, the feller is." Spanish Jack wiped a hooked arm across his face. They were on the edge of a water hole on Arrowhead land. Stoll having been on his way out to have a word with Piggott about this new development, to make certain that the rancher moved no cattle onto Crear land, when he had chanced to meet the Arrowhead foreman. "Yuh'll save me a longer

31

ride," Stoll had said.

"How d'yuh know he is kin o' Crear's?"

"Crear wrote him. Why else would he come? He didn't even know Crear had died."

The dark-visaged Arrowhead foreman eased his black horse forward to allow it to drink. Stoll, standing there thoughtfully, reckoned he might as well go the whole hog.

"Word is that Arrowhead planned to push some beef onto that grass out there."

Spanish Jack's head half turned, his dark eyes glittering, and there was the wraith of a humourless smile on his thin lips. "One way or 'tother, Stoll, it ain't nowhere near in yore jurisdiction."

"I'm the only law there is of any kind in this part o'the country," said Stoll doggedly.

"Sleeman law," said Spanish Jack. "If yuh want to jaw on that issue with Piggott, let me know when it is, because I wouldn't want to miss it."

"Too late now, anyway," Stoll said, "now the Allotts are out there."

Spanish Jack spat onto the ground. "Mebbe they won't stay." His voice was flat, expressionless, but what it said was that Stoll could take it any way he wanted. Stoll chose to let it slide, looking up at the mounted man, seeing the slightly puffy patch below his left eye, the only blow that the unlucky drummer had got in. "Somethin' else eatin' at yuh?" the Arrowhead foreman asked.

Stoll, slightly nettled, thought: *What the hell.* He said: "That feller, the drummer in The Black Horse, they'll put him on the next stage out, but he's shore still a sick boy. It near went too far, Jack."

"No bastard pushes it to me," Spanish Jack said. "Them that don't already know it, has to learn it right off. That slippery bastard LePage been in yore ear about it?"

"No," Stoll lied, for LePage had

33

indeed walked down and, as he had promised Allie he would, had a word. "But some of the citizens are gettin' to be somewhat edgy whenever Arrowhead comes in, these days."

"Them same psalm-singin' bastards take Arrowhead money," said Spanish Jack sharply. "They can like it or lump it. Tell 'em *that*."

★ ★ ★

Even as the Sleeman sheriff and Spanish Jack talked at the water hole, two Arrowhead riders, Orde and Cashman, came out onto the boardwalk from the Ace of Clubs saloon, that stood two doors along from the general store. With the exaggerated deliberateness of the partly-drunk, they stood there belching and chuckling together and from time to time passed remarks about townsfolk who were walking by. Black, in his store, working near the front window, stiffened, and unseen, fixed cold eyes on them, but in the space of a moment, the store at that time being empty of customers, felt the gentle pressure of his wife's slim fingers on his arm.

"They'll go, soon." For a brief time that seemed to her longer than it really was, he failed to respond; then, with a feeling of intense relief, her fingers sensed the relaxation of his tension.

Across the street in the interior dimness of The Black Horse, LePage too was staring out across the batwing doors, the woman, Allie, beside him, while the piano player, Ed Crouch, his ever-present derby that tilted over one eye, rippled up and down his tinny keys and, apparently oblivious, was humming to himself. Finally, still playing runs and without even looking around, he said: "What's going on?"

"Nothing yet," Allie said in a low voice. "There's two of the Arrowhead just come out of the Ace, which sinkhole is welcome to their custom, and they look like mischief."

"Black's watching," murmured LePage,

but if the remark was intended to carry any significance it was lost on Allie. Crouch played on, absently. For a man whose left wrist was deformed, his playing on a piano that was past its best days was remarkable. The malformation was the result of once having had the long barrel of a Colt smashed across the wrist, long ago in a somewhat less salubrious saloon in Dodge City. Sometimes Crouch grinned and made a wry joke out of it: "Now I never fail to play a request from the floor even if I don't know the tune."

Across the street the attention of the two Arrowhead riders had now become engaged by the plodding approach along Main of Fechney's freight wagon with its four-horse team. Orde nudged Cashman and they laughed inordinately loudly, bumping against one another in their glee. When the team drew level with them, both men suddenly took off their large hats and, yelling, waved them, causing the lead pair to shy away in fright. Fechney cursed and at once stood up, hauling at the long reins, calling reassuringly to the horses, almost losing his balance, until, a few yards further on, he managed to get the rig under control again and wound the reins around the brake handle. He swore loudly at the Arrowhead pair who laughed hugely for a few moments; then, as laughter died, began to look at the old man seriously. The half drunk can swing from mirth to anger in the flick of an eye. These two stepped off the boardwalk and shambled along the street to stand, eventually, beside the wagon step.

"Shore am sorry, ol' timer," Orde said, surprisingly, and extended his right hand up towards Fechney who, more in confusion than anything else, grasped it. Orde then simply pulled him from the wagon, then let go, so that Fechney fell heavily onto the dusty street. Shocked, but trying to struggle to his feet he was still off balance when Cashman thrust out one shoulder and bumped him down again.

"Yuh want to watch that bad-mouthin', ol' man," Cashman said.

Over at The Black Horse, Crouch had now joined Allie and his employer at the batwings, but none of them stepped outside. In the general store, Fran had now taken a firm hold on her husband's arm.

"No, Josh! Leave it. They're going, anyway." It was true. Orde and Cashman quite abruptly lost interest in the old freighter, who was now standing and supporting himself by leaning against the side of his wagon. "Stay in here Josh . . . please." Her blue skirts rustled as she herself went quickly outside and presently led Fechney into the store. "You certainly need a drink, Ned, and a chance to catch your breath." The freighter was still somewhat fuddled and made no answer. Outside, the Arrowhead men had mounted up near the Ace of Clubs and were moving off up the street on their way out of Sleeman.

Black fetched a bottle and a shot-glass into the living quarters where Fran had taken the old man, an arm across his shoulders. Black could not look at Fechney, but in any case the freighter was still fully occupied in gathering himself together. But from the doorway of the shop's storeroom, silent, cheeks flushed, the boy Jody watched; and he had seen and heard everything that had taken place out in the street, and his eyes were now on his father's back. Yet when Josh Black turned to stand the bottle on a table, Jody had gone; he had slipped out by the storeroom window and was now scuffing along a hot and airless alley on his way through to one of the back streets, wanting to be by himself for a time, filled with the shameful knowledge that his own father had stood and looked on while an old man, a friend moreover, had been pushed around, maybe hurt, by a pair of drunken cowboys. For Jody, it was as though his world had split apart.

# 3

OLD Fechney had been more shaken than at first he would admit.

"I ain't afeared o' them sort of hombres. Gawd knows I seen enough of 'em in my time, but I ain't as spry as I was. I shoulda druv on, I reckon, let 'em laugh their fool haids off."

Black poured another stiff peg of spirit and put it near the freighter's hand. "Not so easy to do," Black said. Fran insisted on cleaning up Fechney's left hand, for he had grazed it somehow in the scuffle, and in dressing the small area of broken skin. She went quietly and competently about the task, her mouth set in a firm line. Silently she acknowledged that it had been she herself who had restrained her husband from going out to help and she knew he must be deeply ashamed, but there was no opportunity for them to talk right now. Vaguely she wondered where Jody had got to. For his part, Fechney seemed not to have considered why Black had not gone out into the street, if indeed he had seen what was going on.

"You ought to rest here a while," Fran said. "You could stay overnight, go on in the morning. That would be best."

"Do that," Black said, "please."

The old man shook his head. "Ain't that I'm not right obliged fer the offer," he said, "but I got freight to haul out o' Sleeman an' a heap more to pick up at Ritter's Ford, tomorrer, early. A man's got to be there on the day an' around the hour now, for there's plenty others quick to jump in. The freightin' business is gettin' real crowded, what with the railroad pushin' out every which-way, an' all."

They were reluctant to let him go but were loath to argue in the face of the reasons he gave. They did manage to persuade him to take a meal of cold-cut meat and freshly-baked bread, but right after that they walked with him out to his wagon and soon saw him moving slowly along Main and finally out of Sleeman.

Across the street in the Black Horse they also noticed the wagon departing, and when it had gone they talked again about what had happened to Fechney.

"So where was Stoll when he was wanted?" Allie said.

LePage smiled slightly. "Now, there's an irony, my dear. I did have a quiet word with Rufus and he promised he would speak with Piggott. Today, in fact. So while those two fools were up to mischief here in Sleeman, I believe Sheriff Stoll was indeed on his onerous journey out to Arrowhead."

Allie was visibly taken aback.

"My God, that was quick," she said.

"Oh please don't misconstrue the events," said LePage at once. "I feel quite sure that the good Stoll didn't leap to obey my slightest wish. It did become perfectly clear that he had already intended speaking with Piggott about rumours of Arrowhead's moving a herd onto the old Crear range. Now that the young people — Allott I believe is their name — have gone out to Crear's legally, Stoll seemed anxious that Piggott should be told of it without delay."

"Arrowhead," breathed Allie. "Arrowhead, Arrowhead. It's all we ever hear." She looked at him directly. "The drummer is on his feet and packed, but he won't come down until the stage gets in."

"For which prudence one can scarcely bring one-self to blame him," LePage observed. "The wonder to me is that he can stand at all, much less see. He should be grateful for your gentle ministrations, my love."

"Just make sure the stage doesn't leave without him," she said, turning to leave. "For one thing, Jessie wants her room back."

Crouch, a cigarette in one corner of his mouth, ran his fingers lightly over the stained keys. " . . . *When I'm far from home . . . I dream of you, my Mary dear . .* " Humming then, and playing softly, he said to LePage: "Why am I now whipping myself for not going out there?"

"For the same reason," said LePage, "as I. We tend to mind our own affairs at the present time, and that is no bad thing."

"I know." And he sang: "*One day I'll come back to you . . . my Mary dear.*" Then, playing a glittering run, said: "But why do I still feel so very bad about it, Mister LePage? Not that I could've done a lot." He laughed, but without mirth. "Maybe finished up with the other hand junked as well. Then you'd have been out one piano player."

Page merely muttered something.

"I didn't catch that," the pianist said, still playing.

"Black didn't go out," said LePage

thoughtfully. "I saw him at the window, and it happened right out in front of his store."

Crouch flashed him a sudden smile: "Maybe they were good customers."

LePage took a long, slim black stogie from an inside pocket of his immaculate jacket and stood quietly lighting it, — still looking across at the blank frontage of the general store. Then he flicked the dead vesta over the batwings and turned away.

★ ★ ★

Twice every week the stage came through Sleeman, whip cracking, the vehicle creaking, lurching, trailing rich dust, to come hauling up finally outside the depot, the team blowing and streaming with sweat, driver and guard slinging down piled-up baggage and maybe, on occasions, a strongbox for the bank. Not many of the passengers who came in on the stage had any intention of staying on in Sleeman; it was more in the nature of a stopover for drummers and the like, though occasionally a girl would alight, like some garishly plumed exotic bird, to be met by somebody from one or another of the saloons. But no, not a lot of people named the town of Sleeman as their destination, yet it was often-times a busy place. Cattle buyers came, and on odd occasions, some desk officer of the U.S. Cavalry on his way through to Tolliver's to bid for horses. And outside of those who travelled by the stage, drifters passed through Sleeman too, and sometimes a lone, hooped and canvas-covered wagon, ma, pa, kids, and tethered behind, a cow or a workhorse, all heading on through to some promised land over the horizon. Mainly, however, it was the stages that fetched in news of the outside world, a place that some who lived in Sleeman could scarcely begin to comprehend. It was from this source, the stage, that they heard the Barford bank had been held up, though not much was taken, and anyway, those who had done it had been caught, all three, and one of them shot dead; so that was that. And another time word came that William Bonney was dead and had been for some long time past. No doubt there would be more tales about that, and even songs about it. Sometime.

★ ★ ★

Fran Black cleared away dishes and busied herself with other household chores. Josh Black was attending to the wants of customers in the store, but when things got quieter he came through into the house. Neither of them referred again to Fechney. Black said:

"I hear Stoll's gone out to Arrowhead to try to make sure Piggott moves no cattle onto Crear's." Fran's dark blue eyes found his. He thought she seemed tired, somewhat careworn.

"This place . . . " She did not go on, but shook her head.

"Where's Jody?"

"I don't know. Probably with Aaron."

He nodded. Then: "God help those Allotts if they do start sodbustin' out there."

She was well aware of the implications that such a thing would have in these cattle lands, deeply so in view of the fact that the newcomers would have Piggott and his hard Arrowhead men to deal with. "I hope Stoll isn't about to mention the possibility of it to Piggott; of their maybe farming the place."

He shrugged. "I don't know. I can't read Stoll. He blows hot and he blows cold."

"Jody talks with Stoll sometimes."

"When? When did he talk with Stoll?"

"He does . . . sometimes, passing by there."

"When did he tell you this? Jody?"

"It . . . just came up." She now wished that she had not mentioned it.

Someone had come into the store. Tightmouthed, Black went through to

48

see what they wanted. While he was there, the boy, Jody, came in off Main, and his father's gaze followed him as he went by. Jody appeared quiet, withdrawn, as though he would rather not meet his father's eyes. For Jody, it seemed that now, nothing would ever be the same again.

# 4

HE was taller than Jody and ten pounds heavier, but there were some remarks that could not be borne, no matter what the odds; so Jody hit him and they set to, the pair of them, in the schoolyard, where fighting was forbidden, but neither of them giving a thought to that. All Jody Black wanted to do at this moment was to smash away the big, puffy, sneering face of Danny Regan and make the other boy take back what he had said in front of others. Where they were, in a dusty hollow, they were out of sight of the schoolhouse where the strict Miss Tinker was, with her prim face and her probing eyes; and because it was a hollow they could never manage to be far apart without retreating onto rising ground behind them, so once started, both had to go at it willingly, with no

50

time to take a breather. Though Jody was the smaller boy, he was fit and he was just a touch quicker and he had to rely on this speed to leap in and punch and duck away; but whenever Regan managed to land a blow, the sheer force of it shook the smaller boy and took a little of his speed away with it so that he knew he would never be able to outlast the other boy unless he could really hurt him, and soon. Fine dust rose up around the fighting boys until they were liberally coated with it and their shirts were torn as sometimes one boy clutched at the other in their advancing, retreating, ducking, weaving battle. Jody's nose was soon bleeding and a bloody cut had magically appeared, dark through a mask of blood on Regan's left eyebrow. Regan thumped a plump fist into Jody's ribs and Jody wrenched away in pain; then, in a manner his father had once shown him, suddenly shifted his forward-stepping left foot four inches to the right, just as Regan, boring in confidently, threw the next punch. The movement Jody had made was only slight but it was just enough for Regan's fist to go slipping across Jody's left shoulder and for an instant the bigger boy, having committed himself, was off balance. That was when Jody hooked his left hand upward, boring his whole body forward with power from his right foot and he felt the heavy jolt and the sharp pain in his hand as his bunched knuckles took Regan under the jawbone and fetched from him a strange, wheezing grunt, and sent him staggering to one side. Jody, now aware that other children had come, their voices shrilling at the fighters, some calling to them to stop, others urging them on, followed up very fast, pumping left and right fists into Regan's broad face, now beyond caring that his own blows were causing him pain, wanting only to knock that face away, to pulp it; and so he was unaware that Miss Tinker had come to find out what all the noise and the dust could be about, until a strong hand took hold of his collar. Even then, chest heaving, ragged shirt covered in dust and blood, he did not care, for his enemy was down now, rolling, wailing in his pain and humiliation, and that was all that mattered to Jody Black.

"Jody! Jody!" She was shaking him quite violently for he would have flung himself once again at Regan. The faces, familiar faces all around, had now become unfamiliar blurs as he was forcibly pulled away. Alice Kaffnir's was the only one he remembered afterwards, Alice in tears, but he could not imagine why.

So he was taken back to the schoolhouse and by-and-by Danny Regan was brought there too, and he was a mess, Danny was; and he was afraid, too, and everyone would have seen that he was, so that Jody felt warmer and much relieved, and knew that never again would he need to fight Danny Regan.

★ ★ ★

When on the following morning they took time to have a good look around, the Allotts were disturbed to find evidence of recent visitors at the Crear place. On the previous evening they had found the doors of the house open, and in the kitchen, on the heavy wooden table, stubs of candle and burnt matches. These could have been left there by any passing riders, but up on a rise, over a sturdy bridge beyond the stream, it was obvious that a number of horses had been moving around, and not so long ago.

"Cowboys, maybe, from one of the ranches hereabouts," young Allott said. His wife did not answer but was glancing about as though she might be expecting to see horsemen returning. For reasons he could not have explained to her, and indeed would not attempt to, for he had no desire whatsoever to alarm her, he had a strange, vaguely unsettled feeling. There had been that lawman in Sleeman, too; now he had had the manner of a man who had been very surprised indeed to encounter some kin of Dan Crear's and had acted for a moment like somebody on the brink of saying more than in the event, he had.

"Come along, Emily." He led the way back across the wooden bridge, through trees, back down into the yard of the homestead which now was theirs. They went to each outbuilding in turn, discovering little of interest, certainly no livestock of any kind; then across to the cavernous, straw-littered barn where, on the previous evening, they had taken their wagon and lodged their animals. They were about to go inside when Emily pointed further along the line of trees near the creek.

"Look."

They had not noticed it before, but now they walked slowly down to it and presently both knelt and the man said a short prayer. The earth mound had been covered with melon-sized stones and at one end was a very crudely made wooden marker into which had been burned with some kind of iron, DANIEL CREAR, no date of birth, but the date of his death.

"When we can manage it," Emily said, "we must set him up a proper stone there, with a verse." She drew her shawl more tightly about her thin shoulders, though the morning was not cold, and looked around much as, earlier, her husband had done. "I have the oddest feeling, William, that there are other people around, somewhere near, but of course there's no-one."

What she had said caused in him another small tremor of concern, so close was it to the feeling that he had experienced when they were across on the other side of the stream. He dismissed it now, however, and as much to reassure his wife as anything else, he said:

"There's no-one. I expect it was our finding that people had been into the house and some riders had been nearby, that's all. Come along, Em, let's see about getting poor Dan's things out of there and our furniture in. And there are the horses to attend to; and then quite soon we shall need to think about all the things we will have to get, and mainly, find out just whereabouts we might buy a plough."

★ ★ ★

The main street of Sleeman lay baking in the afternoon sun, people moving about at a leisurely pace, old men sitting on benches in the shade, sharing the gossip that had come in on the stage the previous day.

"They do say Billy Bonney's dead."

"Yeah. Killed a whole slew o' people, Billy did. Ten, fifteen, twenty; I don't know how many. Shot Tunstall, he did. Long ago, that was."

"Maw, I reckon he didn't do that, though mebbe he wuz there when it happened."

"They do say it wuz Bonney did it, an' that's when he went to the bad."

"They say, they say. Half the time they don't know theirselves what the hell they say, or where it come from."

"It wuz that long, skinny feller, Garrett donc it. Shot Billy, that is."

"Garrett? Pat Garrett?"

"Wa-al, it's one o'the three tales I did hear, an' it's the one I fancy."

"What about Dave Rudabaugh?"

"What about him?"

"Warn't he there? When Bonney got shot?"

"Maw, I reckon not. I dunno. I on'y heerd about Billy."

"I thought they were friends."

"Dave Rudabaugh an' him?"

"Maw, him an' Garrett."

"Yeah, well, in these here times a man don't rightly know who his friends are. Not after sundown, anyways."

But there was no such gossip and no lethargy over at the Black's. Fran stood the boy away from her, her hands still on his shoulders, the better to examine him.

"Just *look* at the state of you! Jody, who was it? Was it Aaron?"

"No, o' course it wasn't Aaron. We don't fight, him an' me."

"Who, then?"

His father came in, eyebrows raised, expecting an explanation, but the boy did not want to look at him, and stared at the floor.

"Question him later, Josh," Fran said. And to the bloodied and dusty boy: "Come along with me right now, to that pump; and you peel that shirt off, what there is left of it." Shaking her head, the boy silently following her, she soon set about cleaning him up, then fetched salve for his abrasions and found a clean shirt for him to put on. As each minute went by he knew it brought him closer to the questions that he would have to face. His nose hurt, his lips hurt, his salved knuckles hurt quite badly and there were deep aches in muscles that could not be seen. He had made up his mind, though, to stand firm. Beyond the fact that he had been in a fight in the schoolyard with a boy named Regan, they could persuade him to say nothing. It took all of the boy's courage to keep his mouth shut, but he did it, in the face of everything.

"I've seen this Regan boy," said Fran to her husband, "and he's a good deal bigger than Jody, and maybe a year older."

"Who started it?" his father wanted to know. "Did you or did he?"

Jody chose to discount the fact that he had thrown the first punch, for, as far as he was concerned, it had really begun with what Regan had said to him. So he shrugged, looking down. "We got in an argument an' then it just kinda started." But his father was not to be so easily deflected.

"The first punch that was thrown, whose was it?" No answer. "Was it yours?" Still no response.

"Jody, please answer your father," Fran said.

Reluctantly the boy nodded. "I guess."

But try as they might, they could get no more from him. After he had gone up to his room, Fran sighed and said:

"Give him a little time. A night to think about it. He'll come around."

"I just hope it's not what I think it might be," said Black.

★ ★ ★

In the quiet dusk, the two Arrowhead riders, Leech and Geffan, walked their horses through the trees along the line of the creek. There was a light shining from a window.

"Somebody across there right enough," Leech said. They eased to a halt; gloved hands resting on saddle horns, looking at the lighted oblong through interstices of branches.

"Now, where's that bridge?" mused Geffan.

"There." Leech pointed. "Wide enough to take a wagon, is all."

"Then where's the ford? That way, or up there?"

Leech screwed half around in his saddle, peering through the gloom.

"My bet says up yonder."

"Then we'd best go take a look," suggested Geffan, "an' find out what the depth is there an' how wide it is."

"Where it widens out," said Leech, "is where the shallows will be. C'mon." He wheeled his horse and, Geffan following him, began to go slowly along the edge of the stream.

Inside the house, William Allott looked up from his supper, raised a napkin to his thin lips. Emily glanced at him.

"What is it?"

"Horses," William said, holding up one pale hand for quiet. "I heard horses blowing. Not our horses. Further off."

They both sat at their table, listening intently.

"I don't hear anything," she said

at last. But, not satisfied, he put his napkin aside and rose from the table and for reasons he could not have put into words, said:

"Turn the lamp down Em."

Outside, he discovered that she had followed him into the quiet evening.

"There! Did you hear it?"

"Yes."

Undoubtedly there had come to both of them the sounds of horses blowing, somewhere down along the creek, beyond the shadowy line of the trees; but the sounds were a good distance off now, Allott considered.

"Whoever they are," he said, "they seem to be going away. Just passing riders." She drew some comfort from his words and from his tone, but Allott himself had experienced a return of the strange unease he had felt earlier. They stood quietly for a few minutes longer, listening, then went slowly back inside.

★ ★ ★

Miss Tinker, in a plain dark green dress and a suitably sober bonnet, sat straight-backed in the Blacks' parlor, and for the second time she said:

"I have to say that it's not *like* your Jody. And do you know, he absolutely refused to tell me what it was all about. I could get nothing whatsoever out of the Regan boy, either. Mind you, he was in some state at the time, and consequently somewhat preoccupied."

"Is he badly hurt, then?" Fran Black, fetching tea for the schoolteacher, was now anxious.

"Oh, I'm sure Danny Regan will recover well enough," Miss Tinker said. Her small, prim-looking, rather colourless mouth, Black imagined, even hosted the wraith of a smile. "I expect that some might even say that Master Daniel Regan . . . had it coming. He has earned a certain reputation for using his fists too readily. Of course, I have been at some pains to curb that fault, and I thought that I had succeeded in getting through to him. I was wrong."

"Be that as it may," Black said, "we've tried to teach Jody that there are better ways of resolving differences. What happened at the school has concerned us. We want you to know what our attitude is, about that."

"Jody's been acting out of character about the whole matter," said Fran Black. "He won't say what it was about to us, either. That is simply not like him."

"Well," said Miss Tinker, "I thought it best to have a word, perhaps find out if you knew any more than I. As for Daniel Regan, I fancy he will not be seeking another fight with anybody for some while, though I must say I do have my doubts that it will have cured him permanently. In the meantime, however, I believe the school might see a welcome period of peace. Sometimes these things, coming to a head, do have that effect."

The schoolteacher finished her tea and a little time after that, departed, but Jody, having managed to creep

65

close by, had heard everything that had passed between Miss Tinker and his parents. Yet, when Fran Black said:

"I believe we ought to have another talk with Jody," and went to call him, his room was empty and he was nowhere to be found.

Jody went walking through some of the town's back alleys, well away from where people habitually were. Suddenly he had wanted to be off somewhere alone, with not even his friend Aaron for company; like a boy he remembered in Colorado, Mate, who began to get bad pain, more and more pain, until one day he ran off, not daring to tell anyone of it, and hid up among slab rocks above where he lived, as though in running, he might somehow escape from the agony deep in his stomach, him that they found, eventually, and carried home, but who in a few weeks, wasted to a yellow skeleton, and died. Jody's pain of a sort, would not go, either. Yet, like Mate's, it was not something you could run from.

# 5

LEECH and Spanish Jack came out of the Arrowhead bunkhouse to meet Piggott in the yard, and they paused in the spill of light from the bunkhouse door. The big man stood with broad hands on hips and called away into the grey darkness:

"For God's sake hurry it up, Orde! We're all set to go!"

From the direction of the long corral an answering call came and there was the sound, too, of urgent activity among the horses there.

"So," said Piggott to the men with him, "Stoll come out real strong about it?"

"Yuh could say that," said Spanish Jack. "Don't rightly know what way Stoll would jump if it come to a pinch."

"He can jump any Goddamn' way

he pleases," said Piggott heavily. "Way I read it, he's got no say beyond the edge o'that tin-pot town. What goes on out here is cattle business an' therefore none o' his."

"Some do see it different," the foreman commented, "but that don't make it so."

"Stoll don't know what it is to take risks," Piggott said. "Other folks take their risks. I took mine on this place, built it from nothin' an' stood an' fought for it a time or two. It ain't done yet, neither. I got a ways to go yet. Stoll, nor nobody else is gonna get in the way o'that." Orde now arrived out of the gloom, leading some saddled horses, and straight away each man went to his own mount. "Time to get movin'," Piggott said, and swung his ungainly bulk up into the saddle, leather creaking. "Stick close an' save the hosses. We don't need to push too hard, not yet."

★ ★ ★

After sundown they walked all around the yard and even a little way beyond, calling his name, but Jody did not answer. Josh Black closed the shop early and then he and Fran began to search for him seriously and more widely. They checked the neighbouring properties but to no avail, and then Black stopped, and said:

"The blacksmith. Childs. Jody goes down to the forge sometimes to talk with him. I'll go there. You go ask Morrison at the feed and grain. He goes there too." Wordlessly she went.

The smith, the storekeeper thought, must still be working for as he drew nearer he could see clearly the glow of the forge and hear the ringing of the hammer. Stripped to the waist, skin gleaming with sweat, Childs paused and stepped back from his work as soon as Black went in.

"Jody? Nope, not today Josh. Unusual. He gen'rally stops by, well, most days."

Black spread his hands, let them fall

to his sides. "Thanks, anyway."

"If the boy don't show up soon," said Childs, "send word. I'll go out too. Won't do no harm to have another pair of eyes."

Black nodded his thanks and went striding away. As many another in Sleeman had done, the blacksmith regarded the departing storekeeper speculatively. A tall, big-shouldered man he was, a rugged man for a storekeeper, with unflinching eyes, who moved with a lithe, almost cat-like grace. Childs, as others of his calling tended to be, was a strong, muscular man and of a mind that did not suffer fools gladly, but thought that he, for one, would not particularly care to tangle with Josh Black. Yet the word was that when the old freighter, Fechney, had been roughed up, Black must have been well aware of what was going on, but had done absolutely nothing to help. That, if it was a fact, thought Childs, was more than puzzling. Maybe it was not true.

Again, maybe it was, and Black had his reasons. Childs put aside his work and moved down to the back of his forge and picked up a shirt, shrugged it onto his big frame. He thought he might just drift on down to the general store anyway, and set about helping to find the likeable young Jody Black. As he walked along, he could not get the man, the boy's father, out of his mind. What was it he had thought just a short while ago? Unflinching eyes. Yes. And when, on this evening Black had come to the forge, they had been more than that. They had had in their depths a look that was no less than chilling; a look of death.

They quartered the whole of Sleeman, the three of them, storekeeper, his wife and the blacksmith, looking in all the yards and the vacant lots. Fran carried a lamp. They asked people they met on Main, all of whom knew Jody by sight, but no-one had seen the boy recently. Black himself paused outside LePage's saloon. He could hear the sound of many voices in there and the sound of the piano being played and Ed Crouch's reedy tenor singing:

"*Some say it was Garrett that shot him,*
*Some say that his friend blew him down,*
*But I heard it a-right that on that dark night*
*The devil he came for poor Billy.*
*Bill Bonney, Bill Bonney,*
*The devil he came for Bill Bonney . . .* "

Josh Black pushed through the batwing doors and went into the long, crowded, yellow-lit and smoky room. LePage himself, eyebrows raised at the sight of an unaccustomed visitor, came right across. Jody? No. He knew who the boy was of course, and had spoken to him occasionally, but had not seen him anywhere near to the Black Horse that day, either on Main or out back, in the yard. LePage went and asked others on

72

the storekeeper's behalf but no-one had set eyes on    "He's probably just gone off somewhere with a friend," LePage said in his calm, courteous voice, "and forgotten the time."

"Maybe that's all it is," said Black. He did not believe it and suspected that LePage did not either.

At the top end of Main they met up again, all three. Fran had been to Aaron's house but her boy was not there either. While waiting for her husband she had told Childs about the fight in the schoolyard.

"Somehow I think it's connected," she said. "In fact, I feel certain."

"There's one or two empty places down back o' Reever's corral," said Childs. "Maybe we should go look down there."

"But aren't they closed and locked?" asked Fran.

"For a boy Jody's age," Black said, "there are ways in and out of places like that. He's right. We should go there. You come too, Fran, with the lamp."

★ ★ ★

First it was the rumbling, roaring sound becoming louder, gathering in the night that awakened them, but once awake, what caused them greater alarm was the way the very floor of the house began shaking.

"Will, what is it?"

"I don't know! Come quick, follow me! We'll need a light."

The Allotts blundered from their bed, bumping against furniture, fearful now, for the roaring noise was becoming louder, the shaking much stronger, and there seemed to be other sounds, like men shouting.

On the back porch, not even conscious of the chill night air, they did not at first comprehend what was taking place. The night was bursting with noise and movement, something so intense and overpowering that instinctively they shrank back, a cry escaping from the woman as she clutched at the arm of her husband. Flowing like some swift, boiling current through the yard of the homestead, thumping against outbuildings, sweeping away small wooden fences, great gorgon faces flashing whitely, horns clashing, stormed a seemingly endless herd of bawling cattle. The Allotts turned and ran through the house, flung open another door, and still the cattle came, from somewhere up beyond the line of trees along the water, where the water itself was flung, glittering, upward like shards of shattered glass.

"They're coming across a ford up there!" Allott shouted. If his wife had heard what he had said she made no answer, standing ashen-faced, clutching him again. He pointed. Limned against the grey light of the sky was a horseman, there one moment, gone away the next. The buffeting, roaring, bawling mass continued sweeping down and around and through the yard, on and on as though it would have no ending, until the woman, shivering with fear as much as from the cold, sank to the floor, wrapping her thin arms around the legs of her husband, and riven now with sobbing. Then, as suddenly as it had come upon them the tide of beasts went flowing away into the farther darkness, but they could still hear the savage yelling of the night-riders and now, two or three heavy, booming shots. The Allotts did not know it at the time, but those with the herd were now setting about turning it, riding to the wild-running head of it, eventually to swing the leaders around in a wide but tightening circle until eventually the great beasts would begin to mill and settle and there would be no more running that night.

★ ★ ★

In the yard of an abandoned barn on the western edge of Sleeman there had been a ladder, and with it, Black had been able to climb to a loft whose door was hanging by only one hinge. He took Fran's lamp up there with him and in the pale wash of light from it, leaning into the loft, was able to see into every corner. He stood immobile for a few seconds, then quietly said:

"Come on now, Jody. You're late for supper."

There was no movement at first from the huddled figure, and a stab of apprehension went through the storekeeper, then straw that was littered inside the loft rustled, and the boy stood up. His small face was pale and tense, almost as though it had shrunk, and he was slowly rubbing cold hands together. Then he came to the opening of the loft and followed his father down the ladder into the yard.

All through their late supper they said very little, but right afterwards, Black put down his coffee cup and looked squarely at his son.

"Jody, we can't let it go. You know that, don't you?"

"Yes, sir."

"We have to know why you ran off and we have to know about the fight

77

with Danny Regan, because it's all part of the same thing, isn't it?"

The voice was fainter this time, barely audible. "Yes, sir."

"All right then. Suppose we go back and start with Danny Regan. What happened? Did he do something or say something to you, or did you, to him?"

Jody licked his lips, knowing with certainty that it had come to an end, There was no way out.

"He said . . . something." Fran came and brought a chair and sat down softly beside her son. "He said you was a-feared of them Arrowhead riders . . . " It came tumbling out then, bright tears showing in the corners of his eyes. "He said you was a great kind of friend for Mister Fechney to have, to watch him get laughed at an' roughed up right out in front of the store an' . . . an' be too yeller to go out an' take a hand, that's what he said." Jody sniffed and wiped a sleeve at one cheek. "That's when I hit him, I guess."

Black's expression had not altered in the slightest. He nodded. "And today? Today you kind of got to thinking that there really might be something in what he'd said, that right?"

The boy did not have to answer, head down, staring at the table. His mother reached across and put one hand gently on his shoulder, lifted her fine brows to her husband. "Josh . . . ?"

He shook his head slightly, leaned forward, speaking quietly to the boy.

"Jody, there are things . . . things from a long time ago that it's best you don't know. None of them anything to do with Mister Fechney. Nothing to do with Arrowhead or anybody else around here. Not in Sleeman. One day your mother and I will talk to you about it, but not now, not yet. You have to trust us, Jody, that's all I can say. I know it isn't enough, but it will have to do."

The boy nodded, but Black knew it was still no good.

In the raw light of the morning the Allotts, who had slept no more since the cattle came, surveyed the damage. All the outbuildings bore traces of the passage of the great beasts, and splintered wood from low wooden fences, and thin poles from what once had been a small corral lay strewn around; and the earth all about the yard and beyond the house had been chewed into an earth-dark track where the herd had gone pounding through. Wordlessly the young couple followed this trail to where it indeed emerged from a ford across the stream some hundred yards below the homestead. From that place the longhorns had swept towards the house itself, funneling through the yard, then fanning out across the lush grasses of Crear — or rather Allott — land. And there they still were, spread out across the expanse of range, hundreds of them, their great white faces lowered, grazing quietly.

Of the men who had come with them in the night, there was no sign.

"Cattle can stampede," said Allott. "That's likely what happened, Emily. Whoever they are they'll no doubt be back to round them up."

"And to pay for the damage they did," his wife said. Now that the fears of the night had receded, Emily Allott was beginning to feel aggrieved.

"What if we'd been outside; I mean, if it had been earlier in the evening? Will, we might not have been able to get out of the way. We might have been killed."

He sighed and nodded. Not long afterwards he saddled one of the wagon horses and made his way out towards the nearest bunch of grazing cows. They watched him coming with only slight interest, no fire in them any more. All bore the same bold brand, a shape like a slim triangle.

Presently Allott came back to his wife.

"Emily, I'll go into Sleeman. I have

to find out about a plough, and while I'm there I'll speak with Sheriff Stoll and ask him exactly what our rights are, in damages, once we know who owns these cattle. If anyone should come here, the cowboys, tell them where I've gone and ask them to drive the cattle back to their own range." He paused, looking down at her pale, serious face. "Are you sure you'll be all right?"

"I don't want to stay here alone now, Will. I know I said I would; but take me with you. We can lift the remainder of the things out of the wagon and go to town in that."

It took them about two hours to reach Sleeman and when they got there it was afternoon and they went straightaway to Stoll's office. He waved them to chairs but they preferred to stand. Stoll heard them out, evincing no real surprise at what they had come to tell him of the night's events, of the cattle and of the brand on them.

"It's not just a triangle, Mister Allott," Stoll said. "It's the Arrowhead brand." He thought: *Christ, here we go*. He rubbed at his whiskery jaw. "Damages? Yeah . . . damages. Well, there's no harm in tryin' o' course. Frankly, I don't reckon there's a whole lot o' hope." There might be harm in trying but he could not immediately think of a way to tell these people that.

"It's true that the damage isn't great," Allott conceded, "it's, well, the principle of the thing."

"Principle," said Stoll. "Yeah, of course. Well, the name of the rancher is Piggott. Seth Piggott, an' he's, well, somewhat of a hard man, I can tell yuh that."

"We'll go to see him, nonetheless," said Will Allott. "How do we get to Arrowhead from here, sheriff?"

"Er, look Mister Allott, I don't recommend that yuh go out there yourself. Best to let me have a word with Piggott about it an' see what can be done." They stared at him blankly. Finally, pacing up the office and back again, he had to say: "Look, things ain't as straight out simple here as er . . . in some other places; not so cut and dried. It's like livin' on the borders of civilization. People like Piggott hold a lot o' sway. They've had their hard times in a hard country where there's not much law, an' they have to be handled . . . carefully."

"Does that mean that this man is his own law and might well ignore our complaint?" the woman asked. She seemed maybe a little feistier than Stoll had thought.

"That depends," said Stoll vaguely, a mite unsettled by the very direct approach. "Let me talk with him." He walked around his desk and sat in his chair.

Reluctantly they accepted what he had said; and then staggered him by remarking in an off-hand way that they had really come into Sleeman to find out about purchasing a plough.

"A what?"

"A plough."

"Mister Allott," said Stoll, sitting forward in his chair, "is it my understanding that you plan to be a sod — a farmer out on Crear's?"

"Yes," Allott said, "it is. My uncle's place does seem to have fine, rich soil and there is plenty of good water there and some natural shelter from trees. We will soon plant more trees, of course. And we believe there ought to be a fair market hereabouts for fresh produce, which right now must need to be freighted in, probably over long distances, and at high cost."

Coming on top of the cattle affair it was more than Stoll could assimilate, together with the unsavory prospect of having to front Piggott over that.

"We'll bid you good-day then, sheriff," said Allott, "and get about our business, and no doubt you will be in touch with us."

"I believe there's nothin' more certain," Stoll said.

Not surprisingly there was no plough to be had in Sleeman, but the reaction they got at Childs' forge, while it involved raised eyebrows, was more hopeful.

"I could put one together cheaper than you could ship one in, built up," Childs said slowly, wiping his hands on a piece of rag and taking careful stock of the Allotts, "all but the fine steel ploughshare. I could send for a John Deere one, but it might take a little time."

"Then we shall have to wait, there being nothing else for it," said Allott. "It's a pity, but we'll have to accept that all this will take longer than we had thought at first."

Childs had to say it. "Yuh quite sure yuh do want a plough, Mister Allott?"

"Of course," said Allott almost primly, "how else can we set about breaking the ground for crops?"

They had come out of the forge shortly after and along Main to where they had left their wagon, and in fact had almost reached it when a hard-nosed rider from Seeth's Lazy K noticed them and, fresh from being told in a saloon the fast-travelling news that they were in town trying to buy a plough, called to them. A gangly, buck-toothed boy he was, in rough range clothing, with very worn-down boots and a wide brimmed hat that was of filthy appearance. He looked exactly what he was, a drifting cowboy of prickly temper, not overly smart, resentful of his betters, willing to ride for any greasy sack outfit that would take him on, and none too scrupulous in his dealings, if an opportunity arose. Before him he saw two of the kind of people he despised most, young, cleanly though not expensively dressed, owning a wagon and, it seemed, a property as well, and setting up to be dirt farmers. It was too good a chance to let go by.

# 6

THE dirty and ragged range rider let his bold gaze move over William Allott, and his prominent teeth showed, discoloured, pressing into his lower lip. Emily Allott's eyes flickered nervously up and down the street as though she might be hoping to catch sight of the bulky figure of Stoll, but there was no sign of him. One or two other folk, passing, had heard the cowboy call to the Allotts but, after a glance or two, none even paused as they went on their way. Lately, in Sleeman, it had come to be thought of as good sense simply to go about your business and not worry about what might be happening to anybody else.

"So," the cowboy said, coming to a spraddle-legged halt between the couple and their wagon, "they do say yuh're lookin' to buy a plough. Now, ain't that one helluva note? A plough. In cattle country. Mister, whatever it is yuh got a-tween them pink ears o'yourn, it shore ain't a brain!"

"Your opinion," Allott said stiffly, "is of no interest to us whatsoever. Please stand aside." They could smell the rankness of him, standing there in sweat-stained, dark blue shirt, levis and very old, scratched chaps, wide belt and looped shellbelt and holstered Colt. He was wearing a red bandanna, and a sack of Bull Durham was poking out of a torn shirt pocket.

"Like shit I'll stand aside, mister. I wouldn't stand aside fer no Goddamn' dirt farmer if we was all chewin' the fat on the main street o' Hell, so there ain't no chance a-tall o' me doin' it here in this clapped out, fly-blown town."

Emily, cheeks flaming, made to go by him to get to the wagon but he held out one grimy hand.

"Let me pass, please," Emily said.

89

"Yuh must've got some o' that there dirt blowed in yore ears, missy," he said.

"I'll thank you not to speak to my wife in that way," Allott said. His face was pink and he even took a half pace towards the man who was blocking their way. For his trouble he received the palm of the man's hand in his chest and a sudden shove that sent him backwards two full paces.

"Listen to me, sodbuster," the cowboy said, no longer grinning, "yuh think I don't like ploughboys, well, yore boots are gonna burn off when Seth Piggott out on Arrowhead gits to hear about yuh. My bet here an' now is yuh won't stop a-runnin' 'til yuh git clear to Nevada, an' then on'y to change yore pants!"

Emily made as though to move again and now, not content simply to bar her way, the cowboy seized her slim arm and sent her staggering back towards her husband Man of peace or not, Allott could not stand by and see his wife manhandled and he thereupon made to take hold of the other's sleeve, but the young man was unused to such proceedings and the cowboy quite easily braced himself and straightened his arm, the heel of his hand jarring the bridge of Allott's nose. Allott again went back-stepping, then his head went down and his shirt front was at once covered in blood.

Along the opposite side of Main, Black had come into the doorway of his general store and had been watching intently the unfolding of the scene at the Allott wagon. As though reading his mind, Fran came softly to stand behind him as she had when Fechney was being razzed.

"Let it be. Soon, Stoll is bound to notice what is happening."

"Stoll's nowhere to be seen," Black said tightly.

"Josh, don't let what Jody said push you into it," Fran said. He did not answer her. They then saw Allott shoved backwards and, her hand on

91

her husband's shoulder, Fran Black felt him go tense. When the woman was grabbed and pushed also, Black, now beyond calm consideration, moved, and though Fran said: "No!" he did not hear her, or if he did, certainly did not heed her, and was already going with long, easy strides anglewise across Main, his storekeeper's white apron fluttering. When Allott went forward and was stiff-armed and beginning to bleed, Black was three yards away, coming swiftly and, for such a big man, very quietly. As Allott was bending, hands to his face, the dark, bright blood beginning to come through his fingers onto his shirt, one of Black's powerful hands had taken hold of the cowboy. The sack of Bull Durham fell from his pocket to the ground and the rider's terrible hat slipped from his head to hang by its thongs between his shoulders.

"Huh?" Black said nothing, but lifted him up bodily by the ragged, dirty shirt. "Leggo!" Black pushed his own face closer and when he did speak his voice was low, husky and filled with menace.

"Hit me, scum, I don't go backwards." As he said it he released the rider's shirt and the man almost fell, mouth open, grimy buck teeth gaping, but he did manage to say:

"This ain't none o'yore damn' business, mister!"

"I've just now made it my business," Black said, no more loudly than the first time he had spoken. "Now hit me."

The cowboy could not believe what he was hearing. Here was this apron-bedecked *storekeeper* for God's sake, giving him the hard word right out on Main, asking to fight. A storekeeper. Yet there was an iron strength about the man; that was obvious. And he sure was a big bastard. Nonetheless, pride often dictates actions at such times, and the cowboy made his next mistake. He did hit Black. Or to be precise he hit at Black, for when the thin-gloved fist arrived, Black was no longer there, having slid easily to one side. And then in an explosive red flash, something struck the range man in his left eye and his whole body was hammered backward to clump against the edge of the boardwalk and a cloud of dust rose up around him.

Allott was straightening, wiping at his face and at his shirt with a bloodstained bandanna, his wife now in tears, pale hands on him, trying to help him. But it was she who suddenly called: "Look out!" Black spun about with astonishing speed and saw that, though the man he had hit was still on the ground and moving only gropingly, he was fumbling for the butt of the Colt and then tugging at it to free it from the holster. Black stepped to the street, whipped his boot forward, kicking dust at the head of the fallen man, who instinctively turned his face away and then in one instant Black was over the top of him, a boot pressing down hard on the fist that was gripping the butt of the big pistol. Black's weight came on it and the man screamed as his fingers crushed under the press of it and remained numb and unmoving as Black slowly raised his boot and then brought it smashing down again, and this time the scream could be heard even by Stoll inside his office at the jail, and the cowboy rolled away in agony, raising thick white dust, his damaged hand clutched under one armpit.

"Hoy!" It was Stoll at last, jamming his hat on, coming down off the boardwalk outside the jail. "What's goin' on here?"

"You're a touch tardy, sheriff," Black murmured.

"Goddamn it," said Stoll, arriving, "I can't be out gawpin' up an' down Main all hours o' the day!" He stared at the man with the tucked-up hand, now lying in a foetal position and moaning deeply. "Who the hell's he?"

"You might well ask," said Black. "He was starting to shove these folks around for no good reason that I could see."

"We are really most obliged to you, Mister . . . er . . . " began Allott through his bandanna.

"Black," said Black. "He wasn't up to much." He glanced at Allott's wife and said: "You all right, ma-am?" She nodded, but plainly she was shocked and frightened.

"Thank you."

Surprised now, he noticed that Fran had come and was standing nearby.

Stoll was doing his irritated best to get the cowboy back on his feet. When finally he did, as a precaution he relieved the fellow of the Colt. And when he was able to get a look at the rider's damaged hand he glanced soberly at Black.

"Shore made a raw steak o'this."

"We were none of us bearing arms, sheriff," Black said piously. "I for one object strongly to having a gun drawn on me under those circumstances. How about you?"

Stoll flushed, knowing he was being guyed. "We already got one lawman in this town," he said, "an' I'm him."

"Well," said Black quietly, pinning Stoll with a flat stare, "be that as it may, you can't be gawping up and down Main all hours of the day."

Stoll jerked at the cowboy's good arm and favoured Black a final aggrieved look. "I'll talk to yuh later, Black."

"I'm usually at the general store," said Black, stone-faced, "just down there."

Stoll moved his shambling and still whimpering charge away along the street towards the Sleeman jail. Black turned again to the Allotts to find that Fran was talking with them, trying to persuade them to come with her for a rest and a cup of coffee before setting out on their journey home.

"Thank you but no," said Emily bravely, "we have to start back. There's still a great deal to do." Nothing that the Blacks could say would dissuade them. When the Allotts were both up on the wagon seat Emily smiled down wanly. "We will pray for you."

As the wagon moved and went creaking on its way, Black said to Fran: "If what I hear about a plough is true, they ought to be saving all their prayers for closer to home."

Watching the storekeeper and his wife walking back towards the general store, Ray LePage, stogie held between his long fingers, said to Allie:

"Now, that was a most diverting incident, my love."

"What is it about this Black?"

"I truly wish I knew. There is quite definitely *something* about Mister Josh — Joshua, no less? — Black."

"Well, there they go," Allie said. "She looks none too pleased, I must say."

"Would you be," asked LePage, "if I had just gone out from these secluded premises, bold as brass, and half crippled some ragged, buck-toothed half wit in half the time it takes to tell about it?"

"Oh, I don't know," she said perversely. "It might even give me food for thought."

"Then prepare to starve your mind, my dear. My games are all played with my own decks, each one new, pristine, still in the wrapper. And storekeepers should stick to what they're supposed to be doing."

"You sure you don't know Black from somewhere?"

"I'm quite sure I've never set eyes on him before." Neither he had, but he had seen plenty of men like him, who had not been storekeepers. There was definitely something about this man which drew a second and cautious look.

Black did not think Stoll would bother to come, but come he did, late in the day, in fact just as Black was in the act of closing the store.

"You'd best come in."

"Here'll do," said Stoll dourly. He jerked his head. "That feller I got along there is somewhat crippled up."

"There's a doctor up at Kendall," said Black blandly.

"The cowboy says yuh already had 'im," said Stoll, "yuh didn't have to stomp him."

"I make my own decisions at the time," Black said, "in the light of no other advice being available."

"Well," said Stoll, arriving then at what it was he had come to say, "don't take no more hands — or feet — in anything, Black. People kin git the wrong idea, they see the storekeeper comin' bustlin' out on Main, peacekeepin' an' such."

Black fastened him with a hard look. "Why didn't you warn them about what sodbusters can expect from cattlemen anywhere? Let alone what might blow up fast once Arrowhead gets to hear of it."

Stoll flushed. "Look," he said heavily, clearly thin on patience, "I already got my damn' plate full o' Piggott an' his Arrowhead, an' cows druv onto the Crear place at night, or stampeded, I don't know which. At least I think I don't. An' I ain't had no chance yet to talk with Seth about that nor nothin' else. An' I have given them Allotts the word that sodbustin' ain't the wisest thing to be doin'. But either they don't understand that or they don't want to understand it. So I don't need no more advice, nor hindsight, nor foresight nor nothin'."

"Sheriff, would you care for some coffee?" asked Fran from the doorway, almost in a whisper. Stoll's mouth fell open but he shook his head and jammed his hat more firmly on.

"Thankyuh, but no," he said thickly and turned away.

"Now see what you've done," she said to her husband.

"I'll try to do better from this time on," said Black quietly. The only person who seemed pleased about it all when he heard, was Jody.

# 7

THEY took their time going home, both of them tired and very unsettled. Finally it was Emily who undertook to drive the wagon, for on more than one occasion William had had to pause to apply the already sodden bandanna to his swollen nose. His shirt and his jacket were darkly stained with dried and drying blood and his clothes were in a poor state.

"We should never have come here," said Emily dispiritedly. "This is a lawless, terrible place not fit for decent people to live in."

"The man who came to help us could never be seen as anything but decent. Just a storekeeper. He took a big chance, doing that, him and his wife, both."

"Yes. Yes he did, of course," she

said, at once contrite. "I shall always feel grateful to them both for that. But William, why would that awful man, that stranger, want to give offence to us? To lay hands on us? We mean no-one any harm. All we wish to do is work the land, our land."

William was still dabbing gingerly at his nose. "That's just the problem, it seems. From the attitude of the folk in Sleeman, even Sheriff Stoll, though he did not say so outright, except to caution us about our plans,. they strongly disapprove of people who simply wish to farm instead of raise cattle. I've known for a long while that the two make uneasy neighbours, but never knew it could lead to such aggression."

"William, do you believe Sheriff Stoll will speak to this man Piggott about the cattle?"

"I don't know, Em. Yes, perhaps he will. Since he told us so, though, I'm not any longer sure it will do much good. The things the cowboy said to us stick in my mind, and when I consider them against what took place last night I'm given to wondering if it was a stampede after all."

"Do you mean to suggest that those riders drove their cattle onto our land deliberately?"

"I'm afraid I do."

Her face was pale, drawn, and she said again what she had said to him the previous night. "We might have been killed."

"Yes."

They drove along in silence for a time as the dusk came down, the precursor to the velvet night. He reached back into the wagon and found her shawl and placed it about her narrow shoulders.

"We could go home," she said, "leave here. Sell the land."

"Is that what you want to do, Em?"

"You know it's not what I really want. This was to be our new start, Will, with the help of the good Lord."

"Then if you feel you want to stay, we'll stay. What you want to do is what I want. I'm not afraid. Well, yes, truthfully I am; for you, first. But together we can stand firm."

She extended one hand and placed it on one of his, and no spoken answer was necessary. They drove on under the sweep of the heavens.

It was when they came around a curve in the trail, passing between upthrust rocks cut sharply against the night that they saw the wavering glow in the sky. It was not the last light of a sunset, for that was now past, and in any event, was over in the wrong direction. No, this was a rising and falling light and had a ruddiness about it that could mean but one thing.

"Quickly, change places with me!" said Allott sharply.

"Will, the house — !"

When he had hold of the reins he flicked them hard over the backs of the horses and shouted and whistled the animals out of their easy torpor until the wagon began to gather speed, creaking and rocking under the Allotts, their wide eyes fixed on the climbing fire-glow.

★ ★ ★

When Stoll stepped out of his office in the early evening for a breath of air and a stretch, the first thing he saw was the three riders from Arrowhead, Piggott himself, flanked by Spanish Jack and the man whose name he knew to be Leech. They were ambling their horses onto Main. Stoll raised one hand and all three looked and then came easy-moving towards him and drew to a halt only a couple of yards away, Piggott, one hand resting on a hip, Leech with gloved hands on the saddle horn, Spanish Jack beginning to build himself a smoke from a small sack with a drawstring.

Piggott nodded. "Stoll."

"Cents."

"Well," said Piggott then, "were yuh wavin' a greetin' or do yuh want to say somethin'?"

"The second," said Stoll.

"Then git to it. We got plans for the evenin'," said Piggott.

"I hear tell," said Stoll, "that there's some Arrowhead beef got onto the old Crear place. Happened last night."

Spanish Jack was lighting his smoke, the fluttering matchlight dancing across his dark, pocked face. Leech sat his saddle, smiling faintly.

"That's true," Piggott said in his husky voice. "Yeah, that's true. A herd got spooked by somethin'; moon shadow like as not. Nothin' the boys could do but let 'em run for a ways. They'd been movin' 'em out o' the draws an' canyons up near Keswick's, settled 'em near Crear's line, an' then it happened. They forded the water there, an' that slowed 'em some, an' the boys got to where they could turn the leaders. Didn't lose a single head."

"So be it," said Stoll. His expression was giving nothing away.

"That new feller out there didn't

waste no time," said Piggott.

"Mebbe," said Stoll. "So happened he was in town an' mentioned it. Thing is, Seth, are the cows still on his grass?"

"That they are," said Piggott evenly. The horses' heads were moving about and leather was creaking.

"Well, naturally, he wants them off there," Stoll said, "soon as they can be moved."

"If'n that's what he wants," Piggott said, "then that's what we'll do. But Stoll, we'll git it done when we git good an' ready. You tell the boy that. When we git good an' ready. Right now we're here in Sleeman an' we come here a-purpose to lay the dust." He jerked the reins and pulled the horse's head around and his rider and his foreman did likewise, Leech favouring Stoll with a lopsided grin as he went. Stoll, his face burning now, stood on the boardwalk watching all three as they progressed along Main and eventually hauled in again and got down and hitched their horses outside the Ace of Clubs.

★ ★ ★

It was the big barn that was burning, roaring with flame, thick smoke rolling into the night sky, and the fierce heat smote them like a blow as they arrived in the yard, their horses wide-eyed and not wanting to go near it. Allott, in fact, seeing the distress of the horses, turned the team and wagon away and finally brought it to a stop on the other side of the homestead. As they sprang down he called:

"Fetch buckets, bowls, anything we can use to carry water from the stream. The barn's too far gone but we have to try to stop the fire spreading!" Indeed she could see that this was so. Other dry outbuildings stood nearby and the nearest of them was already beginning to smoke. The Allotts both fetched a bucket and fell to the task of dipping water from the stream and staggering awkwardly back, skirting the savage heat pulsing from the blazing barn, to drench the smoking boards of the nearby structure. Trip after trip they made, noticing neither time nor fatigue, nor feeling pain as yet from hands made raw from the weight of water and narrow metal handles. Only when they had done all they could do and when the blaze began to diminish did Emily suddenly cry:

"The horse! Old Ben! Oh Will, he was in there!"

"Oh dear God!" cried William, and he had half started forward in an involuntary movement, a useless gesture, when she grabbed his arm and pointed.

"No, look!"

Wild-eyed, stamping, tossing his head, the old workhorse had appeared at the very edge of the dying light from the barn. He sprang away again into the gloom, but they knew he would not go far. Whether he had broken out of the barn early on, or had been let out, was something they would talk about later; for the moment they could feel only immense relief that the animal was safe. All at once Emily slumped down to sit on the ground, her hair, partly unpinned, hanging in filmy strands, her shawl gone somewhere, her skirt filthy. She was utterly exhausted now that the worst was over. Sparks were still spiralling into the dark sky and stray fragments of glowing straw were drifting about, settling on everything. The one thing that had worked in their favour, all through, was that there had been little or no wind.

"The small table and chairs," Emily murmured as though only to herself. She meant the few remaining items of furniture which they had simply unloaded from the wagon before setting out for Sleeman, to be taken into the house the following day.

"Never mind," he said. "Ben's out, we're here, the house is safe. Now we should give thanks."

Smoke was curling around yellow lamps, and beneath them, men and brightly-clad women jostled, while others sat around small tables where playing cards flickered. It was a noisy, busy night in The Ace of Clubs, the Bar Dogs in their aprons and striped shirts moving back and forth behind the long, mirror-backed bar, setting them up, wiping glasswear, eyes shuttling about, alert always for the loud, angry word or tipped-over chair which would signal the start of trouble; for trouble of that particular kind was far from a novelty at night in The Ace of Clubs. This night in particular they turned their eyes frequently to the hard, dangerous trio from Arrowhead. Nobody in the place stared outright at Piggott or his two men, and certainly everyone in the place took most exceptional care never to bump against any of them in passing. Arrowhead, for its part, ignored everybody and settled down to some serious drinking.

As time went on and the old piano played and the cards were dealt and dealt again and the general din was punctuated by occasional laughter, even those standing nearest to the Arrowhead group began to relax somewhat, some even to converse with them. So the incident involving the Allotts, beginning with their enquiries for a plough, and ending with the arrival of Stoll, eventually came out. Even Spanish Jack set aside his shot-glass and looked.

"Plough?"

"That's what they was lookin' for."

"I damn' well knowed there was somethin' more to it, the way Stoll was so jumpy," said Leech. "Sodbusters!"

"They been talkin' to Stoll a lot," Spanish Jack said.

To the nearer bystanders, Piggott said: "Tell me about what was said an' what went on." They were not slow, a few of them, to curry favour. They related the whole thing in detail for Piggott's benefit, beginning with the buck-toothed cowboy.

"Give 'em the message about the plough, then," said Leech, belching. But the next part of it did not go down at all well with Arrowhead.

"The storekeeper? That Black feller?"

"There ain't no other storekeeper in Sleeman."

"Yuh mean to stand there an' say," said Spanish Jack, "that this Goddamn' counter wiper come walkin' across an' put the boy down?"

"Sure as hell did. Didn't mince matters no wise, neither. An' that ain't all of it by no means. This hombre was on his ass an' somewhat shook up, but purty soon he come to hisself an' was some riled, an' he drawed his Colt; but afore he could git to blow Josh Black's lamp out, that storekeeper feller, he stomps his fingers real bad so folks could hear the feller screamin' all up an' down Main. An' about then, Stoll come, an' by an' by he took that broke up cowhand in to cool off."

"Well, I'll be Goddamned!" Leech said. "That shore has soured this here coffin varnish!" Nonetheless he poured himself another generous peg and tossed it down. And what made it worse, Arrowhead were aware that some men in The Ace of Clubs and probably others elsewhere, had clearly been impressed by what this storekeeper had achieved.

* * *

What transpired the next morning made it plain to the young Allotts that one of them must return to Sleeman as soon as possible to talk with Stoll again. First they came slowly into the yard and stood looking silently at all that now remained of their barn, a heap of blackened trash, blue smoke still spiralling upwards in several places. After that they found that it was difficult to settle down to any routine tasks, even though their losses of personal belongings had not been great, for the fire had been intense, frightening, and for a time all the other buildings on the place had been threatened by it. The sustained physical effort in carrying water from the stream had been sapping, though the results of their frantic efforts had not been apparent right away. Despite the fact that they had fallen into their bed and slept the sleep of sheer exhaustion, now in the light of morning their limbs, their whole bodies still ached. Disconsolately they walked around the smouldering mess that had been their barn, and then for no particular reason, walked as far as the stream. It was down there under the trees, in among brush, that Emily glimpsed something and, stooping and reaching her arm in, pulled out a tin canister. William took it and turned it around, looking for a label, but there was none. He sniffed at the container, then glanced at his wife, eyes widening.

"Paraffin!"

Momentarily she could not reply, for

the inference was something she did not wish to contemplate. Then:

"The fire was set. Will, I'm very frightened. One of us must go back into Sleeman right now to report this to Sheriff Stoll."

"First the stampede, then the fire," William said, "and that terrible fellow in town. What kind of ungodly place have we come to, Emily?"

Pale and seeming almost shrunken, she was still trying to grasp the reality of it.

"They meant to burn us out."

"It's as well they didn't begin with the house," he said. "They must have thought that they had plenty of time, then maybe they heard the wagon coming. Emily, when we got here they must have only just left."

"Or maybe even stayed around to watch," she murmured. Somehow the very notion of that seemed even more chilling. It was then they decided that it would be she who would go back to Sleeman while he stayed on watch.

The previous evening, about the time that the Allotts, physically spent, had been crawling into their bed, Black was brooming the boardwalk out in front of his store and getting ready to close it up for the night. Working by the light beaming from the long front window, he was conscious that the saloons were still in good voice, and he was in full view when Piggott, Leech and Spanish Jack came out of the Ace. Leech was the first to notice him.

"Well now, if it ain't the bully storekeeper hisself."

Narrow-eyed, Black nodded to them but continued his steady sweeping.

"So this is him," Spanish Jack said, his words slurred and his voice tending to loudness from drink. "The hero o' Sleeman." With Leech trailing him he came plodding along the boardwalk, rubbing at his stomach and belching. Piggott hung back, smiling in anticipation.

"It's a real hard town, this'n," Leech said. "Even the aprons come out on the street when the need demands."

Black straightened up slowly, still holding the broom.

"Bet a feller like you could cut a real hole with that thing, storekeeper," said Spanish Jack. Black swallowed hard and made no reply. Without turning his head to look he knew that, hearing their voices, Fran had come quietly through into the store and could also see as well as hear the men from Arrowhead.

"He don't say much, this apronman," said Leech loudly.

"He says more, hear, when the odds are with him," the Arrowhead foreman remarked. A few paces away Piggott chuckled, thumbs hooked in his belt. Spanish Jack came a step closer to Black, staring into his face. Black made to look away but the swarthy man reached up one hand and grasped Black's jaw between thumb and fingers, "Look at me when I talk to yuh. Now, as I hear it, storekeeper, yuh hit a boy.

A boy. Why don't yuh try at hittin' a man?"

Black managed to draw away and as he did so, Spanish Jack lashed a boot at the broom and sent it clattering off the boardwalk into the street. Then he reached forward quickly and pushed Black's chest, sending him stepping back a pace. Now both Spanish Jack and Leech followed him up closely, and in order to avoid them he had to step down off the boardwalk; still they came forward, pressing him, pinning his arms now, and in his twisting struggle to free himself, his white apron fell away and Piggott now ambled down off the boardwalk, stooped and picked it up.

"Dropped yore badge," Piggott remarked. As Black continued struggling even more violently, Piggott dropped the apron onto a pile of horse dung and carefully pressed it down with one boot. The two Arrowhead riders still had hold of Black, shoving him, and now his nose was showing a trace of blood and his shirt had been torn and was hanging loosely from one shoulder. Piggott, now tiring of the hazing however, had gone to the hitching rail outside the Ace and swung up into the saddle.

"C'mon boys; leave the soft bastard to go count his change."

With a final hard shove and a burst of laughter they then shouldered Black heavily and he lost balance and fell in the dust of the street. When Leech and Spanish Jack had gone to their horses and mounted, Piggott walked his own horse forward and sat staring down at Black.

"Take care not to git too uppity, storekeeper," he said, and he dropped the dung-smeared apron onto the face of the prone man. Then, laughing, all three swung their horses away and went on up Main at a canter.

Fran was already coming through the doorway of the general store and other people were emerging from various places; but surprisingly, it was the immaculately attired Ray LePage who strode across the street and made to help Black to his feet. Black hurled the soiled apron away and wiped a forearm across his lower face, smearing it with bright blood from his nose.

"I'm all right."

Nonetheless, LePage would not be deflected and went up on the boardwalk with him, to where Fran stood, all three now in the clear light shining through the store window. Black's shirt was indeed ragged, his torso and one side completely bared, and he was covered in dust and pungent traces of horse dung.

"I'm all right," Black said again.

LePage merely nodded, looking hard at him. Black apparently did not wish to meet his eyes.

"Come inside, Josh," Fran said. "Come in and get cleaned up."

LePage stepped back down into the street and fetched the storekeeper's broom and handed it to Fran. "Goodnight, then."

"Goodnight, Mister LePage. Thank

you." It was Fran who had answered him. He nodded, turned and went striding back across Main towards The Black Horse.

"My," said Allie when he came back in, "aren't you just the gallant one?"

"Leave it, Allie," LePage said.

"Couldn't see much," she said, "but what I did see wasn't nice."

"No," said LePage.

"What's the matter, Ray? Seen a ghost or what?"

He shook his head, his manner towards her unusually discourteous.

"Leave it." Then: "Let's go have a drink."

Ed Crouch at the piano was picking idly, one-fingered, half singing half talking along: *"Bill Bonney . . . Bill Bonney . . . The devil . . . he came . . . for Bill Bonney . . . "*

Going on by, LePage said: "Ed, is that the only damn' tune we're going to hear from now on?"

Watching the departing back of his employer, Crouch raised his eyebrows, shrugged and struck up something else.

"Pay him no need, Ed," Allie murmured. "I don't know what's got into him." Carrying a bottle and shot-glasses she followed LePage through the long, smoky room. Because she was following, she was not in a position to notice that when he paused momentarily to light up one of his black stogies, the hand holding the match betrayed the merest tremor.

# 8

FRAN, working quietly in her kitchen knew, deep inside, what the humiliation of the previous night would have cost him, and she was aware that, after they had closed the store and turned out the lamps, she herself, clumsily, had not improved the situation.

"Perhaps we should leave Sleeman, Josh, sell up and move on."

His face an agonized, taut mask, he had flung down the remnant of the soiled shirt, newly stripped off, and leaned, grasping the back of a chair, chest heaving in his impotent fury. Yet, when he spoke his voice was low, almost a whisper, and it was for her, a well-known measure of the quality of his anger.

"Move on? Where to? To some other damn, fly-blown town like this one? To

125

one more place where there'll be others just like them, like Piggott and Spanish Jack and his crew? How long do we keep moving like that, Fran, and how far do we go, in the finish?"

"Sh-h, Josh . . . please. if the boy hears you he'll come down."

It was but a ploy to calm him down, he knew, for he had not spoken loudly, and the boy in his bed upstairs could scarcely have heard him.

And again this morning, breakfast had been a meal of barely-suppressed tension, Jody alone prattling away as usual, and having to be answered as though everything was normal. Somehow, working in the store later, the elder Blacks contrived, for the benefit of all who came in, an outward show of normalcy, yet Black himself was often more withdrawn than usual as he went about his mundane tasks, for he felt a kind of guilt now, and was reluctant to meet the gaze of people opposite him across the counter; and even the most commonplace of jocular remarks, which ordinarily would have been treated in kind, now seemed loaded with new meaning. More than once during the morning, he had caught himself wondering: "Does this man know what happened? Does he know what I allowed those bastards to do to me? Is there snide laughter when I've turned my back?" Fran sensed what he was thinking and once, in passing, pressed his arm, but there was no answering touch or glance.

A woman from a small outfit to the north of Sleeman came in and bought a number of items, and the storekeeper and his wife carried some of them out for her and put them on the ranch buckboard. They paused to wave her off and watched as the buckboard, trailing dust, went heading on out of town. Black would have tarried a few minutes more outside in the warm morning, but his wife's voice came to him with unaccustomed sharpness.

"Go inside," Fran said. Her tone was deliberately low, but there was about it an almost breathless urgency, and when, instinctively, he made as though to turn and look, she said again: "Go!" This time he moved without hesitating longer, and she followed him in swiftly, skirts rustling. "Didn't you see him?" He realized that her face had drained of colour and now she glanced around nervously to make quite certain that no-one else was inside the shop, strolling among the stacks of merchandise.

"See who?"

"It was . . . I'm certain it was Crane."

Very slowly he turned his face to look towards the bright oblong of sunlight through which they had just come, then back to her.

"Where?"

"Down near Parson's, just come in, by the looks."

"Alone?"

"When I saw him."

"You're certain?"

"As certain as I can be."

"It's been a long while, Fran."

"Do you really think I would ever, ever forget Crane?" Her delicate face was ravaged; she looked suddenly older, and the certainty of what must have been torturing her mind, wrenched at him. Crane. God Almighty. He would rather it had been almost anyone else on earth; *anybody* rather than him.

"If it is," he said, "the best thing we can hope for is that he's just riding on through." She knew quite well that he was now doing his best to assuage her fears, but the attempt was transparent; yet she humoured him to an extent, and even managed to smile at him. But when he looked into the blue depths of her eyes he saw that there was no true light in them, as though the very life-spark had died.

It did not take long for word to come, passed on in all innocence by customers.

"Been a real hard-nose in town, askin' fer an old sidekick, name o'Spanish Jack."

Of course. Spanish Jack. A man of

the same stripe, dangerous, but not anywhere near as dangerous as was Crane.

"Give a name, did he, this man?"

"Nope. An' nobody asked, neither. Didn't look to be the kind that'd take kindly to it, but there's a real firm opinion that he's Dave Crane."

"Who's he?" Black asked, stone-faced.

"If yuh don't know, then I'd say yuh're well off."

"If that's the case I reckon I'll not push it." Then: "Still in Sleeman, is he, this man?"

"Naw, somebody pointed him to the trail to Arrowhead an' that's where he's headed." And added: "Didn't surprise nobody that he'd been a friend o' Jack's, but I shore hope he ain't plannin' to stay around these parts."

Not long after that, Fran, talking with another woman along Main, saw the Allott wagon come in and draw up dustily outside Stoll's office. She was surprised to see that it was Emily, alone, and that she was obviously distressed, clambering down, catching her skirt up and tugging it free in sharp vexation. She hurried into Stoll's office.

Back at the general store, Fran said to her husband: "She seemed very upset."

"Whatever it is, it's not our concern," he said.

"Both of them are new to this country," Fran said. "Frankly, they're not made for the life out here. Perhaps I should try to find out what's happened, see if there is anything I can do. She is very young, Josh."

He drew a long breath. "Jody will be here for a meal soon." That was true. The mid-day break at the Sleeman schoolhouse was at hand; and indeed they soon heard the piping voices of children, and in an exuberant, shouting burst, their son came bounding in off Main.

"Hey Ma . . . Pa! Did you hear? Did you hear what they're sayin'? They reckon he was here!"

"Who?" Fran asked with sinking heart, knowing quite well what he would be about to say.

"The gunman, Crane! Dave Crane, the Texan! He was right *here*, Ma, in Sleeman!"

"Well, imagine that!" she said in mock alarm. "Whoever he might be." She clapped her hands along behind him. "Wash up right now, before you eat." She followed him through to the living quarters.

Left alone, Black felt the weight of despair come down on him. After a year in Sleeman he had begun to feel a loosening of tension, but now, in a single stroke, it was all back with him.

\* \* \*

Stoll managed to get her to a chair before her legs went from under her; then he fetched a glass of water.

"Jes' take it easy, Miz Allott. Slow down an' start over."

"Our barn," she said. "They burned our barn."

"Who? Who burned it? Where's your husband? Is he hurt?"

She shook her head, took a deep, restoring breath. "But he's alone out there. After what has happened . . ."

"I'll have to ask yuh to explain it to me real careful. The barn burned."

"Yes. There's nothing left, but we stopped the fire spreading. Sheriff, it was a *set* fire; we found an empty paraffin can."

Stoll pursed his lips, leaned his rump back against the desk, not liking what he was hearing and resolving not to rush matters. She went on: "First there was the cattle coming onto our land, and still there, and now someone has burned our barn, and if we had not arrived just when we did, they might have burned us right out. Why would anyone want to do these things to honest, Godly folk?" He knew she was matching up the two events, as indeed he had, but he cursed inwardly;

he had no desire to confront Piggott again so soon.

"I know what you're thinkin' Miz Allott, but the law has to have proof."

She pressed a hand to her forehead. "I do know that, and we're not the kind of folk to accuse others falsely, but after . . . the cattle and that terrible man here in Sleeman, now the fire . . . and the *hostility* we could feel over wanting to work our own land . . . " She trailed off and seemed to slump in the chair as though her energy had deserted her.

"Well," said Stoll carefully, "what you've told me is sure food for thought, an' as a responsible lawman, that's what I'll have to do; think about it, an' then decide what to do — " He moved his bulky frame off the desk and went to her, for it seemed that at any moment she might fall to the floor; and he was a man immeasurably relieved when the office door opened and Fran Black came in.

"I saw her arrive," Fran said, "and she seemed upset." To Emily she said:

"Sit quietly, and when you can move, you're coming home with me for a while. We'll put the wagon in our yard." Emily nodded absently, finding that she no longer had the strength to protest.

Fran made up a bed in the parlour, made rich broth which she persuaded the young woman to take, then advised her to lie back and rest. "You're exhausted, Emily. Josh will go out to your place and explain to your husband what's happened." But she would not rest until she had told the storekeeper's wife all that had taken place, and about their suspicions, their outright fears. To Fran Black it was a story that had all the signposts of worse trouble to come, but she had not the heart, right now, to say as much to this weary young woman.

Less than an hour later, Black crossed his yard, unhitched the horses from the wagon and installed them in the barn. He then emerged with a horse of his own, a bold-looking chestnut with a white blaze on its nose. The storekeeper was wearing levis, dark blue shirt and shallow black hat. From the kitchen doorway, Fran said: "Take care Josh."

He nodded. "Be back around sundown I guess. Keep her here." He walked the horse out of the yard.

People on Main glanced at him and some called greetings as he went by, storekeeper Black out to exercise his horse, as happened from time to time. Stoll, though, still brooding over the unsettling news the Allott woman had brought, stepped closer to the dusty window of his office as Black went by. Off to tell Allott, no doubt. There had been a whisper or two, today, that Black had got a roughing up from some of the Arrowhead. Well, if they had slapped him around, and gotten away with it, they would be back for more sport. Stoll made an impatient noise and turned from the window, thinking about Black. Just now, mounted on a good animal, there had been something about the set of him, he had again given Stoll pause. To himself, he muttered: "Sometimes the bastard don't *look* like a storekeeper."

# 9

LePAGE definitely did not require the burden of the knowledge which he believed he now had. His manner since the previous night had led to more crisp words from Allie. Now she had left him in a room over the saloon, a stogie in one hand and a stiff drink in the other. He now had time to think quietly about what he ought to do. One option was to do nothing at all, certainly say nothing, taking for himself advice he had felt constrained to give to Allie and to his employees: "Keep your heads down. 'Yes sir, no sir, three bags full sir.' We are not here to become embroiled in other people's arguments." He blew a thin stream of blue smoke towards the ceiling. On the other hand he must weigh the responsibility of saying nothing, and maybe have a powder keg explode, see the situation develop and get out of Stoll's control. For if it happened, and it happened on the streets of Sleeman . . . LePage sighed, stood up, drained the last of his drink, walked to a peg and reached down his pearl-grey hat.

He found Stoll in his office and the sheriff looked at his visitor pouchy-eyed as he came in off the bright street.

"I've come to tell you something that might be right and might not. All I want is a few minutes of your time."

Stoll indicated a chair but LePage declined. He felt nervous energy that only pacing back and forth would dampen. Stoll sat listening moodily to the start of what he had to say, but soon leaned forward, questioning sharply. LePage shook his head.

"I don't *know*. But hear me out. Years ago I was in Texas; Fort Worth. Not for long, as it happened; but while I was there, word came in that made everybody who heard it, listen. It was about the deaths, in El Paso, of the Paraine brothers; the Paraines and another man, called Kruger. Real wild men they were. It was all in the "papers soon after, because it was *some* news."

"Heard of 'em, o'course," said Stoll. "Who didn't?"

The saloon-keeper took an irritating time to light up a stogie, then, through drifting smoke, he continued: "Three men down and dead, the Paraines and one other, Kruger; it was said that another got away, though that was somewhat confused. There seems often in such affairs, more than one version to emerge. The man who did the killing — I'm not clear on whether he was a marshal or not — this man was also hit quite badly, knocked down off a flat-deck wagon that he'd been standing on. Hit twice at least in his left side, .45 calibres." Stoll's hard little eyes held LePage. "Now, this man, badly shot though he was, got himself up again and went right at the Paraines. He hit Bob Paraine twice, once in the groin, once in the chest, and though Arvin was still standing, this man just came on, still shooting, and caught Arvin in one eye. And then he managed to kick in a shop door, and it was in there that he killed Kruger."

"So where's all this leadin'?"

"A while after that, the word was that a fourth man with the Paraines was a real bad bastard whose name was Crane. Dave Crane." Now he had Stoll's attention, all of it, in clock-ticking quiet.

"Yuh sure about all this?"

LePage trickled smoke from his mouth, raised one eyebrow. "Who can be sure about anything in this wicked old world?"

"It was a good while ago an' a long way from here," said Stoll.

As though the lawman had not spoken, LePage said: "You might know, last night there was a scuffle up along Main. The storekeeper got roughed up somewhat by some of the boys from Arrowhead."

"I heard," said Stoll.

"I saw it," said LePage, "well, saw some of it, and went across afterwards. Black was in some kind of mess, but not badly hurt. They'd covered his face in dung. Humiliating. Well, his shirt was torn almost right off, and that was how I came to see the marks."

"Marks?"

"Scars," LePage said. "In his left side. I'm not a man of violence, Rufus, far from it, but I've been in some rough corners in this unbridled country and I do know old bullet wounds when I see them."

Stoll's little bean eyes hunted around the face of the man standing, hands clasped behind his back, stogie held between his very white teeth.

"You're connectin' him up with El Paso."

"I am. Two distinct wounds, he had, and at the time the 'papers were most precise, there being an appetite for that sort of detail, and they had come from large calibre slugs. Do you now recall the name of the man who killed the Paraines, and Kruger, in El Paso all that time ago?"

Stoll recalled all right but it was a little time before he said the name, and even when he did, it was a hoarse whisper. "Jim Fallon."

"Precisely," said LePage. "Stoll, Crane was here today. If I'm right about Fallon, then Sleeman, quite soon, might become a very good town to be out of."

Stoll slumped back in his chair. His pudgy face now had a sheen of sweat. "Black — or whoever he is — rode out a good while back."

"Armed?"

"No. No, I reckon not. I assumed he was on his way out to see that Allott boy. His wife was here an' near fainted away, so Fran Black took her in."

"Then let us devoutly hope that's where he's gone," LePage said.

"Christ!" Stoll said. He got up out of his chair and reached for his hat.

Fran Black was mildly surprised to see the sheriff for he did not often visit the general store, and she was even more surprised when he did not offer her any kind of greeting, but said: "Yore husband, Miz Black. Gone out to Allott's?"

"Yes."

"Yeah . . . well." He seemed oddly relieved but his expression was still tense and there was an unaccustomed urgency about his manner. "When do yuh expect him back? Soon?"

"He thought about sundown. Why, Mister Stoll?"

"I have to talk with him," Stoll said, suddenly awkward, but staring at her intently. "I'll keep an eye peeled for him; but if you see him first, tell him that, will yuh?"

"If I see him first," she said, "I'll fix his supper."

Stoll fidgeted a moment, then turned on his heel and went clumping out. Fran almost felt like smiling, but the next instant the feeling dissolved, for

144

the boy came through from the house looking lost.

"Where's pa gone? What's happening?"

* * *

They were in Allott's kitchen and the smell of burnt wood and straw still clung all about the place.

"Your wife has been most kind," Allott said. He looked drained, worn out. His visitor had to say it:

"This isn't your kind of life, Allott."

"That has been made abundantly clear!"

"I didn't mean the cowboy in Sleeman, or for that matter, Arrowhead. This is a hard, cruel land; those who survive in it have to be born to it."

"We want to stay," Allott said. "Getting this place was, well, a new chance." He leaned forward. "We do *know* something about farming, though perhaps we don't look like farmers."

"The cattle lands are not the best place to plant crops."

145

"I understand that," Allott said, "but this is a free country."

"In the end, Allott, whether it's fair or not, face the fact that you might have to stand and defend your place with something heavier than a bible . . ."

"I'll not carry arms."

"The men who will oppose you — who oppose you already — don't have the same scruples."

Allott might have replied but they heard horses coming into the yard. He stood up and went to the porch. There were four of them out there, horses stepping nervously, heads wagging, the big man, Piggott, his foreman, Spanish Jack, Leech and another man dressed in dark clothing, a man maybe touching forty, with dead eyes and a scarred upper lip. Piggott indicated the chestnut hitched to the porch rail.

"Visitor?"

"My business," Allott said tautly.

"Mouthy bastard," Leech said, but Piggott held up one hand for quiet.

"Come to make yuh an offer, Allott."

"I'd hoped you'd come to remove your cattle from my land."

"Take my offer, boy, an' I won't need to do that, for the offer is to buy yuh out."

"The place is not for sale."

"That's a mistake. Around here, people don't take to sodbusters."

"Somebody made that point in town," Allott said, "and again last night when they burned our barn."

Leech sniggered. "Lucky it warn't yore ass got burned."

"Does that mean you know something about the barn?" Allott's eyes were bright with anger, forgetting how dangerous these men were.

"Why, yuh damn' — " Leech began, but Spanish Jack cut in.

"Leech an' me an' Piggott was all in Sleeman last night, an' that's well known. Watch that lip o'yourn yuh fancy little sodbuster or yuh'll damn' soon git it split." Allott was about to say that there were doubtless other

147

Arrowhead men who had not been conveniently in Sleeman, but the swarthy man had begun to edge his mount forward.

Leech said loudly: "Whup the bastard, Jack!"

"Whup me first, Jack." The man who now spoke was filling the doorway, hands hanging at his sides, big-shouldered, slim-hipped, a man who now, in levis, blue shirt and black hat, looked a world away from the man in the white apron, so that for a tick of time they seemed not to recognize him. His eyes were fixed, not on Arrowhead, but on the fourth man, whose head came up slowly, distorted lip pulling back from his teeth.

"Knew we'd meet again one day, Dave."

Leech recovered first, looking across at the dark-clad rider. "Yuh know this here lily livered bastard?"

"Leave it!" Crane's voice lashed across whatever else Leech had been about to say. Taken aback, the

Arrowhead man blinked and flushed slightly. "If this is the hombre yuh told me about," Crane said, "he's no damn' storekeeper by trade, an' his name ain't Black." He had spoken quietly but they had heard every word. Even Piggott did not interrupt. Spanish Jack still sat his horse near to the porch, over the top of Allott. "His name is Fallon, Jim Fallon."

Piggott said: "What?"

"He cain't be," said Leech.

"He is."

"Been a long time, Dave," Fallon said.

"Long time," said Crane. He had a soft but carrying voice. He sat his saddle, one gloved hand on his left hip.

"I still carry the marks," said Fallon.

Spanish Jack half turned his head, questioningly.

"From before our trails crossed, Jack," explained Crane. "Years back, in El Paso; the Paraines an' me an' Jack Kruger."

149

Piggott gave him a quick glance. "The Paraines. By God, yes — "

Fallon turned his gaze full on Spanish Jack. "Back that damn' horse off; I can smell it an' I can smell you, an' I don't fancy the stink of either of you."

The Arrowhead foreman raked fierce eyes across Fallon, who carried no gun, and there was no way he was about to eat crow here on this sodbuster's place in front of these other men. But something in his attitude warned Fallon. Powerful arms reached up, hands gripped his vest, and Spanish Jack was off balance and being hauled over the rail of the porch. Allott sprang out of the way as the foreman's long body came down.

"Watch the bastard!" Leech shouted, his horse slewing sideways, crowding Piggott. It had happened very fast, and now Spanish Jack was between Fallon and the men on horses, the barrel of his own Colt laid against his ear. "Gimme some room!" Leech was bawling.

"No, leave it!" Crane's voice was

much louder now.

"Tell the bastard to draw," Fallon said softly to Spanish Jack, "an' I'll cauterize both your ears at once."

"Back off! Back off!" Piggott was shouting, his horse wild-eyed with the sawing of the bit. To Fallon, he called: "This ain't the end of it, not by a longshot!"

"When the time comes," Crane said icily, "he's mine."

"Don't count on it!" Leech snarled. To Spanish Jack Fallon said: "Go climb back on the horse. The Colt stays here with me. If you want it back, come an' get it from, say, The Ace of Clubs."

"When I do come," said Spanish Jack hoarsely, "if yuh want to go on livin', don't be there."

Fallon cocked the Colt, the sound seeming loud in the warm stillness. To Piggott, now, he said: "By sundown tomorrow, have every head of your beef off this place. Come near this house or the people here, an' the whole country won't be big enough for you to hide in. If yuh don't believe that, ask scar-lip there." To Crane, he said: "Yuh want me, Dave, yuh know where I'll be. In Sleeman. It's where I live."

"It's also where yuh'll die," Crane said softly.

Fallon made a movement with the barrel of the pistol, and grudgingly they turned their horses and made their way out of the yard. Before they all disappeared through the trees near the bridge, the two men on the porch saw the dark rider, Crane, turn his face to look back. Then he too rode in among the trees. Allott took out a bandanna and wiped his face. "I don't know what to say. Will they move the cattle?"

"Probably not. But they'll maybe not bother you again until they've been to town to deal with me."

"I can't have you fight my battles," the young man protested.

"I'm not doing that. Dave Crane was bound to see me sooner or later.

That's all between him an' me an' was as certain to come as sunup. Piggott will use that to advantage, maybe even back him in Sleeman when he comes. You're a praying man, Allott. Pray that I take Crane an' that Arrowhead then backs off, for if I don't, you take any offer Piggott makes you an' then get to hell an' gone out of this country."

# 10

STOLL had seen him coming because he had made damn' sure that he would. He walked out onto the top of Main in the ruddy glow of the low sun and stood there waiting, thumbs hooked in his belt, for the incoming horseman, who was in no particular hurry. Eventually Fallon drew rein and sat looking down at Stoll.

"Yuh know why I'm here," Stoll said.

"I know," said Fallon.

A few people paused, shaded eyes against the sun's glare, looking towards the lawman and the storekeeper, but no-one was close enough to hear what was being said.

"Yuh seen Allott, I take it?"

"I've seen Allott. The Arrowhead cattle are still on his grass an' what's left of his barn's still smokin'. I think he ought to sell up an' pull out. He thinks he ought to stay. While I was there, Arrowhead came, Piggott, Spanish Jack and Leech. Piggott wants to buy that land, he says."

"How was Piggott? Was he reasonable?"

"No, he was bloody unreasonable, an' Leech was pretty bad, an' Spanish Jack was the pure bastard he always is. Crane was there too. He's some kind of old sidekick of Jack's, it's a small world."

"Crane. He was with the Paraines in El Paso," Stoll said.

Fallon moved to steady the chestnut, which was restive. He offered Stoll no evidence of surprise. "He was there."

Stoll made some sort of impatient noise, shoved his hat back, scratched his thinning hair. "Yuh'll go to him, or he'll come here. Which?"

"I'll not push it. So he'll come. El Paso's been like a burr to Crane."

"An' Arrowhead?"

"Jack, for sure. Leech too I think.

I don't know about Piggott. Maybe Piggott too."

"Christ!"

"Whether Piggott comes or not, he'll not let the Allotts alone. You can do what yuh like about it, Stoll, I've had enough. I've seen 'em walk over too many people, an' I've been shoved to the limit an' past it."

"I'm the law — "

"Yuh can't run with the hare an' hunt with the hounds, Stoll."

"Damn' it Fallon, I ain't done that! I got to keep a — a balance, somehow, an' it ain't easy to do."

"It's not even possible," Fallon said, "not with men like Piggott. If yuh don't know that now yuh never will."

"Well," said Stoll, "now the whole damn' thing is gonna come right into Sleeman."

"Something was always going to break in Sleeman one day soon," said Fallon.

"Well," said Stoll, "I'm not about to let it go, just like that. I'm gonna go

talk with Piggott. An' I want a word
with Allott as well."

"Suit yourself."

"You see it as a waste of time?"

"I do."

"I can't sit here an' wait an' watch
it happen. I got to try."

Fallon shrugged. "That's your
business, but I wouldn't kill your
horse getting it all done tonight. They
won't come tonight. If Arrowhead do
come in with Crane, they'll come
tomorrow."

"They won't git this far," said Stoll
resolutely.

"Watch how yuh go," Fallon said.
He had an uneasy feeling about
what Stoll was about to attempt.
"Yuh don't really know Dave Crane.
Whatever happens, don't let him push
yuh."

Stoll nodded curtly, turned on his
heel and stumped away into the gloom,
for the red sun had gone completely.

* * *

157

Fran listened again when the sound of a horse came, but it went right on by.

"I feel . . . responsible," Emily said. "If I'd not come into Sleeman, your man would still be here at home."

"No," Fran shook her head, stood slowly wiping her hands on her apron. "No, don't blame yourself Emily, because you can't ever begin to know all of it. Why and how, all the detail, doesn't matter now; but whether you and William had come here or not would have made no difference at all. We came a long way too, Josh and I, but for reasons altogether different from yours. There were things . . . we wanted to leave behind us, we thought forever, places, certain men. Yesterday one of those men came riding into Sleeman. He went out to Arrowhead. Maybe he's still there. When Josh comes home we have to talk about what we must do; stay or go."

"I don't understand," said Emily. She looked less tired today and some colour had come into her cheeks.

"Be thankful for it," Fran said. "You've got a good man and you've lived a christian life." Once again she went to a window, but there was still no sign of her husband. Crane. The man with the scarred lip. It chilled her even to think about him; and in the whole sweep of the western lands it was to this small town that he had chanced to come, as though some malevolent spirit had guided him to where they were. There was a moment when she felt almost fatalistic, tired of running, tired of hiding, tired of lying, of living a lie. And it was even worse now; there was Jody. He was older, becoming more aware, asking more questions. Emily, holding a curtain aside, said:

"He's coming now, Fran."

She felt suddenly nervous, half relieved, half angry at his being so long away, smoothing her apron, though, patting her hair like some young bride when the latch clicks. He seemed to take an interminable time seeing to the horse before he came in. They were both waiting for him in the kitchen. Fran's finger tips went to her lips when she saw the pistol jutting from his waistband. To Emily he said:

"Will's all right. He's more concerned for you than for anything else." To Fran: "Where's Jody?"

"Up in his room doing some schoolwork."

He told them then about Arrowhead and about Crane. Fran's face went ashen as she listened, and hopelessly she said: "We could go."

"No time, Fran, even if that was the answer."

"When will he come?"

"Not tonight. Tomorrow. Neither you nor Jody must go out of this house tomorrow."

The old, frozen hands of death had taken her by the shoulders.

"Might Arrowhead move against Will?" Emily now wanted to know.

"Stoll is going out to Arrowhead early tomorrow, and he plans to call

160

on your man as well. Best yuh stay here until Stoll comes back." He moved closer and took Fran's hands in his own. "I'm sorry. But if it wasn't here in Sleeman, it would be somewhere else. I was a fool ever to believe otherwise." It was an echo of her own fatalistic thoughts only a short while ago, and though her head sank down and bright tears glittered at the corners of her eyes, she nodded.

"I know. I know."

* * *

In the first grey of the morning, Fallon filled a tin bowl with cold water and washed himself, then dried thoroughly with a thick towel. He dressed in dark levis and a clean tan shirt and went quietly back upstairs. From a locked cupboard he took out a thickly-loaded shellbelt, a worn holster and a long-barrelled pistol that had been kept well oiled. He broke out the cylinder and one by one fed in bright brass loads,

161

five of them; the hammer would rest on an empty chamber. As he worked he wondered whether Stoll was yet up, and wondered what might happen if and when he rode onto Arrowhead.

Fran awakened, and with her first sight of him now wearing the heavy shellbelt and pistol, the holster tied down, came for her the piercing stab of the reality of this day. No bad dream this time. In an instant the years fell away, and what remained was the old, living nightmare. She slipped from the warmth of the bed, pulled a wrap on over her nightdress.

"Crane . . . is he — ?"

"No." Speaking quietly, he said: "Keep the store shut. Keep Jody in, and Emily. She might want to go back out to Will. Persuade her not to."

About the time that the Fallons were talking, Stoll was on his way out of Sleeman, heading along the trail which, eventually, would lead him to the place where he would branch off to Arrowhead. Before leaving, Stoll had spoken to the very few people abroad on Main at that hour and to each of them he had said: "Take real care today. That feller Crane might come into Sleeman. If he does, keep out o' his way. An' if he does, he'll be lookin' for only one man. Yuh know him as Black, down at the general store, but he ain't, he's Jim Fallon. That's right, Jim Fallon, so fer Chrissake keep out o' *his* way. Pass the word." And he had not tarried to offer any further explanation, nor to witness the town's general reaction. An hour and a half along the trail, sweating freely, Stoll hauled up and used both gloved hands to shade beyond the wide brim of his hat. He had been right a moment or two back. It was dust and it was rising from a party of horsemen who were heading towards him, but not yet close enough to identify. Stoll wiped his face with a bandanna and walked the horse forward along the trail, in no hurry now. Whoever they were, he would allow them to come to him.

# 11

THEY were the same four that had been at Allott's place the previous day, Piggott, Leech, Spanish Jack and Crane, and they reined in alongside Stoll, who took a good look at Crane and did not like what he saw. Touching forty, he was lean and muscular, exuding a sense of pent-up power; and there was a distinct menace about him. Scar-lipped, he returned Stoll's scrutiny with a dead, unswerving stare out of dark eyes.

"Well," said Piggott, "what's on your mind, Stoll?"

"I reckon yuh know what it is," Stoll said.

They all wagged gloved hands at the flies darting around men and animals under sweltering heat.

"I bet he's been talkin' to Fallon," Spanish Jack said.

"I've seen Fallon," Stoll conceded.

Spanish Jack said: "He's got some property o' mine an' I aim to git it back, first thing."

So this is the way it would be. There could be no doubt at all that Crane was now going in for Fallon, and now Arrowhead, Stoll considered, had shown its hand. Backing Crane, there was a very high chance they would take Fallon, then they would turn their attention back to Allott. Coming right to it, Stoll said: "Them cows still on Allott's land?"

"They are that," Piggott said.

"The boy don't want to sell, then that's his business," Stoll said doggedly. "Now I got to ask this. You're all headin' towards Sleeman; is it to see Fallon?"

"Yes, it's to see Fallon." This time it was the soft drawl of the darkly-clad Crane. "Him an' me got unfinished business. By sundown today, it will be."

"The town's my responsibility," Stoll had to say.

"Then why ain't yuh in it?" Leech said.

"Leech, yuh allers had a lot to say," said Stoll. Then to Piggott: "Got to ask yuh to turn around an' go back to Arrowhead. Trouble in Sleeman means folks that ain't a part of it are like to git hurt. Worse, mebbe." He shifted his gaze back to Crane. "This here ain't El Paso, an' I don't give a spit in hell fer what there was 'twixt you an' the storekeeper. Didn't start here an' it ain't gonna finish here. That's my last word on it."

"They don't pay yuh enough for this," Piggott told him.

"But they pay me regular," said Stoll. "So what's it to be?"

It was not a good situation. They had not tried to conceal anything, and now here he was with four of them, well out of the way, all of them armed, for Spanish Jack had got another pistol. The angles were bad, too, for they were beginning to shuffle their horses backwards so they were no longer crowding him; but he knew that was not the reason for it. They were giving themselves room, should he choose to push it. Spanish Jack was farthest to the left of him, then inside him, Piggott; Leech was directly to his front, while the most dangerous one, Crane, was across to his right.

"Come on fer Chrissake!" Leech said, irritated by the heat, by the flies, by Stoll.

"No," said Stoll, "wait . . . " His gloved left hand held the reins and was hooked on the saddle horn, and in speaking, aiming to make one final plea to Piggott, he shifted his right hand from his thigh, to raise it, palm forward, but as soon as Crane saw it move, he called:

"No yuh don't!" and drew so fast it made even Arrowhead gasp. The rolling thunder of the gunshot came, Crane was swathed in blue smoke and Stoll was punched violently sideways, yet incredibly, did not fall out of the saddle, but swayed, then slumped forward over the neck of the horse. All the mounts were spooked, Stoll's too, heads sawing, skitter-stepping, but still Stoll clung on. There was bright, dark blood though, all over his shirt and on the neck of his horse and down its right leg.

"He moved for it," Crane said, still holding his pistol.

"Didn't think he was that stupid," Piggott said.

Stoll's horse had begun to jog away, his big body still on it, hunched forward, head nodding limply. After a few paces his hat fell off. Crane holstered his pistol and then he and Arrowhead all came back together and continued their journey towards Sleeman.

★ ★ ★

William Allott had risen early for his sleep had been fitful, knowing that the offer Piggott had made was not so much an offer as a threat. The very stench that still hung about the place was depressing, and before long he made a decision to go into Sleeman. If Emily felt well enough he would fetch her back and then they would decide once and for all what they must do. He knew that, stored in one of the outbuildings, was a bridle and a saddle that must have belonged to Crear and, awkward though he was, he managed to saddle the workhorse. The animal had a rather ponderous gait and it would take some time to reach Sleeman, but Allott did not care. All he was thinking about now, was seeing his wife once again.

★ ★ ★

The town itself had gone deathly quiet for the word left by Sheriff Stoll had spread.

Emily asked Fallon again if he thought Crane would really come, and perhaps others. He nodded. "Crane will want to get it done, now that he's seen me; an' Piggott will want to play the advantage, if it turns out that there is one. I just hope that if Stoll sees them, he does nothing foolish. He doesn't know Crane as I do. Stoll won't stop them. He'll no doubt go across to talk with Will afterwards."

Fran said: "Stoll would have been more use here in Sleeman."

"Maybe; maybe not." He shrugged. "He's in something of a bind. I feel almost sorry for Stoll. Whatever he does, it could look like the wrong thing, afterwards."

Jody had been excited and naturally curious. "Pa, was you really in a shootout in El Paso?"

"It was a long time back, boy, a part of the past. Don't make gods of men who carry guns. Men like Will Allott are worth more than all of them rolled into one." Flushed with excitement and fear and pride, however, the boy's wide eyes seldom left the steel and plain wood butt of the big pistol on his own father's thigh. Diplomatically, Emily took him upstairs to look over some of his school work. When they had gone, Fran could keep up the pretence no longer. Her head went down and her small frame was racked with sobs. He held her. Her head was moving from side to side.

"How can we . . . be here . . . talking as though . . . everything is just normal?"

"Fran . . . "

"There'll be too many, even if Stoll should come back soon."

"It's too late now Fran. There's no going back. If it hadn't been Crane it would have been some other, and if not Sleeman, some other place."

"How stupid we were to believe we could leave them all behind and — "

"Listen."

There was some kind of commotion somewhere out on Main. Fallon went to a window. He turned back to face her.

"They've come."

* * *

As some other people pulled aside curtains, LePage came striding, long-legged between near-empty tables in The Black Horse, for Ed Crouch, standing with the batwing doors held open, had said something.

"What did you say?"

"Bunch of horsemen at the top of Main. That'll likely be them."

LePage joined him. "Any sign of Stoll?"

"Can't tell. Don't think so."

"What's going on?" Allie, in a cream blouse and bright blue skirt, had followed LePage.

"Arrowhead's here, but we can't see Stoll anywhere. If they come here, don't provoke any trouble no matter what. And nobody go out in the street while they're in town. Allie, make sure the girls understand." Crouch and Allie departed. LePage reached for one of his stogies.

* * *

Fallon settled the shallow-crowned hat on his head. "Time to go. I'll slip through the yard."

"What if they come here and don't believe you've gone?"

"If it comes to that, open the shop door and let them see inside. I doubt if even Crane would harm anybody here."

Her face drained of colour, she nodded, laid one hand gently on his arm and turned away. When she looked again he had gone, softly, quickly. Just as swiftly Fran picked up her skirts and went upstairs to where Emily and Jody were. The boy's eyes were still alight with his new knowledge.

"Has he gone out to meet 'em?"

"Jody, have you forgotten so soon what he said to you?"

Deflated, the boy knew he must say it for her:

"Don't make . . ."

"Gods."

" . . . Gods of men who carry guns."

"Yes. Jody, your pa *is* Jim Fallon,

and you can be proud of him, but he meant every word of that. He wants you to remember it and live by it. We came here with you to make a new life, to get right away from men like Crane, and . . . " She trailed off, inclining her head, listening. Then: "Stay here."

She hurried from the room and down the stairs.

They were out front and it was Piggott's heavy voice calling: "Fallon!"

Slowly Fran came on through the store among the stacks of merchandise, trying to get close enough to the large, partly-checkered front windows to see exactly where they were, but without being seen herself. She could distinguish three of them: Piggott, Leech, Spanish Jack, all afoot, all with pistols drawn, standing in a rough semi-circle just out beyond the middle of Main and facing the general store. Crane, she realized, must be off to one side, just out of her range of vision.

Again Piggott called: "Fallon!"

Fran swallowed hard, tried to steady

her breathing and went slowly across to the big main doors and reaching up, slid back the upper bolt, then stooped and slid the lower one across, making plenty of noise about it, She heard someone other than Piggott say something right after the sharp sound of the bolts, but could not hear what it was; then she closed her eyes briefly and opened the door.

Piggott and Leech were the first to see who it was in the doorway, and Piggott raised one of his hands in a gesture which clearly told others to wait.

Piggott said: "Jim Fallon in there, girl?" Fran eased right into the doorway. Now she could see not only Piggott and Leech but Spanish Jack and, along to his left, Crane. Crane's pistol was still holstered, jutting from his thigh. All four men were standing still, looking towards her, and as far as she could see, nothing else was moving on Main except for the four horses hitched outside The Ace of Clubs, tails switching at flies. "Answer me," said Piggott.

"Your man in there?"

"No. No, he isn't."

"She's lyin', I bet," Spanish Jack said.

Fran shifted her eyes to the Arrowhead foreman. "I said he's not here and he isn't."

"Mouthy little bitch, ain't she?" muttered Leech.

Fran lowered her gaze, cheeks burning. She knew she must keep her tongue in check. It was the hulking Piggott himself who came forward carefully, Colt tilted upward, his large shadow moving darkly before him. He motioned and Leech came forward too, cocky-looking, full of himself. Spanish Jack stayed where he was out on Main, but half turned his body to look down the street; and Dave Crane did likewise, to watch in the opposite direction. These had the hallmark of moves that had been planned. There was no sign whatsoever of Sheriff Stoll.

Piggott, dusty, sweating, stinking, came up on the boardwalk, the thongs from his greasy hat hanging loose on either side of his broad, coarse face. Leech stepped up beside him, his bold eyes frankly appraising the slim woman in the doorway.

"If he's got any sense," said Piggott, "he really has long gone, but to make sure of it, we'll take a look."

"As you please," she said, and moved back into the store.

Piggott came in, boots heavy on the board floor, then Leech who contrived to brush against the woman as he went by. Fran made not the slightest movement; nor did she betray any concern as she watched the two ungainly range men, hung with metal and leather, in old, grimy clothing, carrying their sour stench with them, go bumping through her house. When, upstairs, they encountered Emily Allott, Leech said: "So yuh got the sodbuster's woman here."

"Made yore man a good offer,"

Piggott said, "but he ain't seen reason yet . . . No matter; when we git done here we'll go talk with him ag'in. I got the feelin' he'll come 'round."

"If he sets his mind on staying," Emily said, surprising even herself, "then that is what we will do."

"Huh!" said Leech. "Nother sassy bitch."

Fran had her hands tightly clenched, almost praying that Jody, glowering at them from where he sat on the floor, would say nothing, particularly to Leech, that would anger the man. But the boy's mouth was set in a straight line, even though his eyes were afire. Finally the Arrowhead men satisfied themselves that Fallon was nowhere in the store or the house. As they went clumping down the stairs, Piggott said to Leech: "Go out back an' take a look around all the outbuildin's."

Following them, down, hearing this, Fran felt a pang of concern, for it had occurred to her that Jim might well have taken temporary refuge out there, while waiting to see if they did in fact come into the house, perhaps reluctant to move far from his son and his wife. When Leech had gone out and Piggott was again at the front, shop door, she could not resist saying: "Why are you doing this? This isn't your fight. It's between him and Dave Crane." Piggott half turned to look down at her. She could not know how Piggott now saw it, this bold opportunity for Arrowhead; but now that a man like Fallon had come to light, presenting such a hazard in backing Allott as he had, to Piggott the move was plain, even inevitable. Fallon must go. And if, by some chance, he did manage to take Crane, then he could not be allowed to survive. Piggott himself must be the man who would hold sway in all the territory, which meant in Sleeman, too, in the years ahead. And of course, she could not have known about Stoll. So Piggott simply gave her a long look but did not answer her, striding away across the boardwalk onto the bright street where Spanish Jack and Crane were still waiting and watching.

"Took yuh long enough," Crane remarked. "Where's Leech?"

"Checkin' around out back."

"Fallon musta lit out. Mebbe he's gone back to Allott's," Jack said, swatting at flies.

Piggott seemed about to answer him when there came the boom of two shots, one almost atop the other.

"Leech," Crane said without emotion.

Spanish Jack would have gone trotting off along the alley alongside the general store, but Piggott said: "No! Wait! We got to circle wider. Crane, that way. Jack, come with me."

Fallon had allowed Leech to see him, and it had been the Arrowhead man who had let go the two shots that sent splinters flying from dry boards on the barn. But when Leech came cautiously to the place where he had seen Fallon, the man had vanished.

# 12

THE workhorse was a plodding animal that could not be hurried unduly, and in any case was resentful of both saddle and rider. After a while Allott had given up trying to urge it on to greater effort. The heat was oppressive, like a weight on his back and like a weight, too, his deep anxiety about his wife and about their situation here. And he thought about the man, Fallon, come out of his anonymity as a storekeeper and who had had a startling effect upon the hard and genuinely unnerving men who had visited him on the previous day. Reduced to a spectator of events and able to hear all that had been said, and in spite of their bluster, their eyes had told the young man something else; hard and frightening though they might be, they would all walk most carefully around this Jim Fallon. By no means a man who approved of violence, William Allott had nonetheless begun to harbour a phantom hope that, should real trouble erupt, Fallon might prevail. Hollowly though, remembering the odds, he acknowledged that he was more than likely indulging in some wishful thinking.

It was as he drew near to a bend in the trail that eventually would bring him to Sleeman, that he pulled the horse to a halt. He had heard what he believed to be a gunshot, rather dull and heavy, a booming kind of shot, he thought perhaps from a revolver, not a lashing crack of a shot, as from a rifle. To the best of his belief it had come from country away over to his left among rocky flats that were, in many places, thick with brush. And it was, he knew, the fringe of the Arrowhead range. Allott sat there in the pulsing heat, expecting, perhaps, to hear more noise, but as the minutes dragged by and none came, he even began to wonder if he really had heard a shot, anyway. He was in two minds. He wanted to press on into Sleeman and — if indeed it had been a shot — he was curious enough to want to discover the reason for it. At the back of his mind he had a fleeting belief that Jim Fallon had now come to another confrontation with the Arrowhead men, and if that were so, then he, William Allott, surely owed it to the storekeeper of Sleeman to find out if he was all right. Resolutely then, though not wishing to ride across the Arrowhead range, he urged his sluggish mount into motion once again, turning off the trail and presently weaving in and out between boulders and clumps of thorny brush. The sky was clear and blue, only a chalk-mark of cloud across the shimmering horizon, and the sun's fierce blaze seemed if anything to be worsening. Allott, however, kept doggedly on. He had progressed maybe three quarters of a mile and, his nerve wavering, was about to turn the horse and head back the way he had come, when he saw the other horse. It was standing, head up, ears pricked, perhaps fifty yards ahead of where he was, and there was something wrong with the shape of it. Allott ran his tongue between dry lips and began to move hesitantly towards the strange animal. He was less than thirty yards away from it before he realized what he was looking at. The other horse had a rider, but the man, bare headed, had slumped forward against the neck of the animal, his arms hanging down on either side, a bulky man by the looks of him.

Allott had not dismounted but halted alongside the other horse with its limp cargo. He thought Sheriff Stoll was dead. There was a lot of partly dried blood all down the side of his shirt, over his right leg, and down the right foreleg of the horse. Slowly Allott reached across and placed finger tips on the neck of the solidly-built lawman and to his astonishment felt a faint pulse. Swiftly he glanced about.

Nothing stirred; the whole land was inert under the baking heat. Allott agonized over what he ought to do. He had no medical skills and in any case, Stoll was obviously a very heavy man. If he were to manage to get him off the horse to bandage his wounds, he would never be able to get him back up into the saddle again afterwards. No, somehow he had to take him, just as he was now, into Sleeman. There might be no doctor there — and he thought that to be the case, for the storekeeper's wife would surely have called him in to look at Emily — but some of the women might be able to do something for poor Stoll. What Allott did do was reach over and undo the man's bandanna, then remove his own. He wadded them together and managed to push them in under Stoll's shirt, where the red-black wound was, then tuck the shirt back into the waistband. He would have liked to search around for Stoll's hat to give the man proper protection from the blazing heat but felt that such a search would be hopeless, so settled for turning the man's shirt collar up to cover the back of his neck. Sadly, he wondered if the precaution was really worth the effort, for he truly believed that Stoll was dying.

* * *

Fran Fallon moved restlessly through the house, pausing to look through each window, and now, for the third time, came to the kitchen windows which looked out across the yard. Nothing stirred there. The man, Leech, must have searched the outbuildings and departed. Jody, refusing to be contained any longer, was now following his mother around, asking questions to which she had no answers. "Where was pa goin', first off? What did he say?"

"He couldn't say where he would go, Jody. You must see that he couldn't. He has to be free to move. He must . . . Oh, you don't understand." And she could not explain to him, for her stomach had tightened with dread and she had to clasp her slim hands together to try to control their trembling. How could she explain to the boy what was really happening? How could she utter to her own young son the words that were running through her head? "This is how it begins, the stalk, like some terrible dance of death, soon enough booming with gunshots, men calling, long silences, and the dreadful agony of not knowing."

Emily came down. "He wouldn't stay up there, Fran."

"No matter." She gathered the boy to her, pressing his head into her apron.

There came two booming gunshots somewhere outback.

Across the street Ray LePage was also pacing about, burning to know what was happening. Even Crouch was anxious and had ceased fingering his piano keys.

"Fallon," Crouch said again. "I heard his name so often, years ago, then nothing. I thought he must be dead. Do you see anything?"

"No," said LePage. "Come on, let's have a drink."

"What's this?" Allie said. "You? A drink at this hour?" He did not even answer her but fetched a bottle. There were no customers at all in The Black Horse, and for once there seemed nothing else to do. He wondered where the hell Stoll had got to. Then they heard the gunshots; some way off, they thought.

★ ★ ★

There was an abandoned shack alongside a small corral that was no longer used and Fallon, moving fast, got in back of the shack, casting about for some object to throw; he picked up a small stone and flung it among some garbage cans opposite him, at the back of a grain and feed and next to The Ace of Clubs. Leech heard it as he was intended to, and followed up quickly.

Fallon knew that he would have to use speed and caution with Leech, whose shooting, only moments before, had surprised him; so he was well away from the shack and the corral, and at the corner of an alley beyond the grain and feed when Leech, moving lightly for a sizeable man, looking alert and determined, came abreast of the shack and suddenly saw Fallon again. Fallon hurried to the other end of the alley and glanced up and down Main. Arrowhead had disappeared, gone towards where the shots had come from, he guessed. Turning, he was in time to see Leech arrive, throwing down; but Fallon, side on, came down more deliberately, fired once, and Leech whipped around sharply as though struck by a sledgehammer. Fallon slipped out onto Main, knowing that he had hit Leech hard.

Leech was down, right enough, struck in the right hip bone as he had begun to line on Fallon, and because the severity of the blow was such that it at first numbed him, he could not know that the hip-bone, shattering, had also deflected the heavy slug and it had torn across to lodge in his lower spine. Then quite soon he felt the pain.

They all heard it, Piggott, Spanish Jack, Crane, arriving from different directions near the back of The Ace of Clubs; Fran and Emily inside the house, and the boy; even LePage and his people across the street, and others in the town heard it, the sound of Leech screaming in his fiery agony. No longer human-sounding, it must surely be the shrieking of a soul already moving towards the ferryman of Hell.

"Jesus Christ!" Piggott said. "Some bastard's hit."

Fran whispered: "My God, what is it?" Her palms were pressed to her cheeks. Emily's eyes were closed and her lips were moving soundlessly in prayer.

★ ★ ★

Allott on his slow horse, leading the other with Stoll still slumped on it, was nearing Sleeman. Half a mile or so out, he had just heard, with alarm, what could only have been gunfire. His mind flew first to his wife and then to Fallon. Now, too, the problem of where he might find help for the badly wounded Stoll, was becoming more immediate by the minute. Allott was dry in the mouth, tired, with an ache behind his forehead. As he came down off a slight rise in the trail, the town lay before him, and at first glance it seemed utterly deserted. There were though, he perceived then, faces at windows and in doorways, and as he came abreast the farthermost building in Sleeman, a livery with a large pole corral behind it, where horses were moving, he caught sight of a paunchy man in old levis and a reddish vest, making urgent arm motions.

"Git off'n the street if'n yuh got any savvy! Arrerhead an' some gunman an' the storekeeper is at it hammer an' tongs!" Allott drew to a halt.

"I've got Sheriff Stoll here, badly shot. He needs a doctor."

"Ain't none," the man from the livery said, "'cept forty mile away in Kendall. Barber might look."

"What?"

"'Long thar, man! Mitchell, the barber. He's taken a bullet or two out in his time. Best yuh go 'round the back."

Allott saw where the barbershop was and urged his horse on again down an alley next to the livery, where the man was pointing. As the horse bearing Stoll went by him, the liveryman said:

"Looks daid to me."

Allott got stiffly down out of the saddle and, holding the reins in one hand, approached the back door of the barbershop. He had to rap several times, loudly, before a voice asked: "Who is it?"

"Allott's my name. Sheriff Stoll has been wounded. He needs help quickly. I've got him here."

A curtain moved and Allott caught sight of a narrow, bony face looking out. A bolt slid back and Mitchell came out. "Don't know if I can do anything. Let's get him inside, anyway. All hell's broke loose somewhere up Main." He flicked another glance at Allott. "You shoot Stoll?"

"Indeed not! I found him just as he is now, on Arrowhead land."

Mitchell gave him another keen look, then jerked his head, "C'mon then, quick."

In the house behind the general store, Emily was trying to reassure Fran, though she knew that it was but a gesture. The boy, Jody, had vanished.

# 13

FOR as long as he lived and no matter where he went, Jody Fallon would always remember that day, when his pa buckled on the long pistol, and the gunman, Crane, someone from the half-remembered past, came to Sleeman, and Arrowhead with him.

Jody, going quickly but carefully, arrived in back of Gerber's Hotel, about halfway along Main. He knew exactly where he was going, having done this before in the company of his friend, Aaron. A climb to the top of an outbuilding gave access to a short, sloping roof over the kitchen, and from there he could reach the bottom of a ladder attached to the back of the hotel, fixed there in case of fire, and within moments he stood on the flat roof of Gerber's. He crossed to kneel behind the low parapet that overlooked Main. Right away Jody glimpsed his father, down on one knee near the mouth of an alley across the street, next to the Wells Fargo freight depot. No sign of Arrowhead, but there was still some noise coming from someone hurt back there near The Ace of Clubs. The boy went back across the roof to see if he could see what was going on there. He could make out hats moving, some men grouped around an object on the ground. Soon after, the sound stopped. Now he could recognize that these were his father's enemies, the bulk of Piggott and the sombre clothing of Dave Crane, at least. He realized that he could not have missed them by much and had been lucky not to be seen as they had moved towards where the gunfire had erupted and to where the man had been screaming. They were on the move again. Lightly, he went across the roof to the front parapet. Cupping his hands to his mouth, he yelled:

"They're comin' pa!"

Because, but for the few hitched horses, Main was deserted, he had no doubt that his father would hear him; and he knew, too, that there was a grave risk that Arrowhead would pinpoint where the call had come from. Jody tried not to think about it. When he saw them emerge on Main there was no sign of Spanish Jack who, he thought, had been with them in the yard; only Crane and Piggott could be seen, walking quite slowly maybe four yards apart, both with guns drawn, both watchful. His father had gone from the freight alley. Feeling suddenly chilled, Jody wondered where the awful Arrowhead foreman had got to. Maybe at any moment he would appear on this very roof. Piggott was continuing to walk circumspectly along the centre of the street. Crane in fact was now pacing backwards, examining with deliberate care the parapets, the false front along Jody's side of the street. That did it. The boy was desperate to get off this roof and from here on, rely on his small size and his knowledge of the town to keep out of their way. Minutes later he was along at the end of Sleeman near Stoll's office and almost opposite a livery, and just in time to see Piggott entering the very alley where, earlier, his father had been crouching. To Dave Crane, Piggott had made a circular motion with one hand, indicating that they should circle and come together at some place behind those buildings. Piggott and Crane having disappeared, the boy's heart leaped when his father came into view right between where they had separately departed from Main. Fallon, gun in hand, backed slowly into the street, and it was then that the boy also saw Spanish Jack. Having obviously worked out where the boy's warning had come from, he must have gone into Gerber's and up the stairs, and by some means come out onto the roof; but now his whole attention was on Fallon, who, clearly had not seen him. Jody screamed: "Gerber's roof!" And even as Spanish Jack began the deliberate swinging down of his arm to fire, Fallon spun and weaved very fast to his left and shot once, twice, one slug banging noisily into the parapet, the other catching Spanish Jack in the solar plexus and travelling upwards, spreading as it went, tearing at his insides, to lodge deep in his chest. The force of it lifted the man, jolted him brutally, then his body swung half around and he fell, hat spinning away, pistol bumping onto the roof, over the parapet and down into the street. Jody ducked away. Fallon ran across Main and was out of sight by the time Crane and Piggott came back and went to where the Arrowhead foreman lay, dust still hazing around him. Jody ran around behind the livery and along behind buildings on that side of Main, startled faces glimpsing him from windows as he went, until he arrived behind The Black Horse saloon. By the time he stole along the side of that place and peeped out on Main, Piggott and Crane had also gone, perhaps following the way his father had gone. Maybe they had heard something. He must find out. He had got but three paces into the open when he heard a bellow and saw that the huge and ugly Piggott, having outsmarted him, had stepped onto Main some forty yards away and on the same side of the street. Turning, Jody tried desperately to retrace his steps but in his panic, slipped; in the event it was the slip that saved him for, boy or not, Piggott fired at him as Jody dropped, the breath driven out of him. Vaguely he heard Piggott calling:

"I got the little bastard!" And another voice, Crane's, shouting from further off:

"Never mind him! We can get Fallon boxed!"

Piggott crossed Main and there was another booming shot from him and a sharp smacking sound and a gasp near at hand; then someone gathered the boy up bodily and the world became light and shadow, swinging crazily as he was carried at an awkward jog-trot off the sun-bright glare of Main, through doors and into dim coolness. A woman's voice said: "Put him down over here. Oh, my God Ray, you're hurt!" Jody was trying to focus on the people who had gathered around him, but it was a minute or two before he could do so, still gasping for breath; but when he did, he could see a woman with painted lips and who smelled of some sickly-sweet perfume, a thin man in a derby hat, a much larger man with a checkered cloth draped over one shoulder, and the one who owned The Black Horse, LePage, his splendid grey suit with a lot of blood on it. Jody said:

"They're huntin' my pa! He's Jim Fallon . . . "

"We know, son," Ed Crouch said. "Take it easy. Allie, see what you can do for Ray; he doesn't look at all good."

# 14

FRAN FALLON was almost rigid with fear. "Emily, I'm sure it was Jody's voice I heard." The two women were standing in the long kitchen, unable to sit while, outside, gunshots were booming, voices shouting, horses whickering. And earlier there had been the dreadful screaming from someone badly hurt. Now, Fran's mind was made up. She would go through to the shop door to see if she could catch a sight of any of them on Main. While she was reaching to slide back the second bolt, she gasped as there came an urgent knocking on the outside. When the door swung open, Allie, a woman from The Black Horse saloon was standing there.

★ ★ ★

Fallon himself had almost come full circle; he was down on one knee near the abandoned corral shack, pulsing with sweat, yet alert for the slightest sound of their approach, and beset with awful fears for the safety of his boy. There had been unaccountable gunfire on Main. Balanced against this was the knowledge that two of them were down, Leech dead, certainly, attended only by flies, just out of sight of where Fallon was. Spanish Jack was likely finished too; yet, but for Jody, Fallon himself might be already dead. He tensed, listening. They were coming. He could hear the heavy thumping of boots on hard-packed earth. Piggott. Crane did not move like that. Crane was a goddamn' black cat. Quite suddenly and much closer than he had thought probable, from among lumber and boxes in the yard, Piggott called: "Too bad about yore whelp, Fallon! He pushed it too close!"

The words struck Fallon like physical

blows. That had been the gunfire he had heard. Realizing that his whole body had knotted up, he forced himself to regain control. With Crane somewhere near, to lose concentration was to invite death. Slowly Fallon began to edge his way backwards until the lowest pole of the corral pressed against his back. He bellied down, resting on his elbows, gun still gripped in his right hand, and eased under the rail. The sun hammered at his back, flies darted; at any moment he expected to see his adversaries coming. He was in fact across the width of the corral, on one knee, when they did come, Piggott from the right of the shack, Crane from over to the left, the latter moving very fast, crouching, and it was Crane who first tumbled to what had occurred and yelled at Piggott: "Down! He's backed off! Down!"

Fallon fired across the empty corral and though Piggott flung his heavy frame back behind the shelter of the shack, Fallon could not tell whether or not he had hit him. The darkly-clad man, Crane, had vanished. Fallon had to make a quick decision. Behind him was open range. To retreat further would be suicidal, yet it would be equally fraught with risk to close on them blindly. Hit or not, Piggott had stayed behind the shack. What about Crane? Fallon had to draw one of them, and it had to be Piggott. Thirty yards to his right was the remains of an old wagon, long abandoned. There was no point in delaying. He set his sights on the derelict and went for it, arriving in a flurry of unavoidable dust, and to utter silence. If either of them had seen him go, there had been no audible call between them. He allowed his breathing to settle before giving his whole attention to the shack. Yes. There. Where the shadow of the structure should have been cut cleanly, a curved shape disturbed the symmetry. Piggott. Fallon stood up and ran towards a point several yards to the right of where the Arrowhead rancher was, going quickly, making no effort at stealth.

Not a little alarmed at the sounds of someone running in, Piggott, one large hand already covered in dark blood, started half up and was in time to see Fallon coming, and only five yards away by the time he looked. And that was all he had time to do before the double explosions erupted and the two mule kicks struck him, one in the chest, one in the belly, and sent him down, this time for good, in a welter of blood and a cloud of white dust. Twenty five yards beyond Piggott, among some empty casks, Crane fired in a swirl of gunsmoke, but was well wide as Fallon ran on and gained refuge at the corner of an alley. Not pausing even for an instant, he went right on through and out onto Main. By the time Crane came almost casually out, Fallon was between thirty and forty feet from him. Crane came to a halt, stood still. Fallon had been vaguely aware of faces over near The Black Horse, one of them, he thought, Fran's, but he dare not take his eyes off Crane, standing with his boots planted slightly apart, long pistol hanging by his side, as was Fallon's own.

"Long way from El Paso," Crane said.

"You should've stuck around," said Fallon. "Kruger an' the Paraines were so taken with it, they're still there."

Crane nodded. "Point made. You should be there too. You was twice hit."

"Not my day to die," Fallon said.

"Maybe today, then," said Crane in his soft voice.

"Maybe. Tell me, what brought Arrowhead in?"

"Piggott warn't well pleased to find out about you. It didn't fit in with plans he had even with Stoll gone."

"Stoll?"

"Stoll's shot. Dead, I reckon. Out on Arrowhead."

Fallon felt sick. Now he badly needed to know about Jody; but Crane said:

"Let's git it done." Even as he spoke his pistol was coming up very fast; but Fallon's right shoulder had dipped even as he twisted side-on, and the long Colt banged and bucked, belched smoke, and Crane, incredulous, was hit solidly, his long body slapped backward. His right arm, with the heavy pistol, swung away to one side as though he was trying to maintain balance on a tightrope. Another flash and boom of sound and the second one caught him, higher than the first, up near the throat, and sent him, head back, heels slipping, hard down on his back. With the pistol gone, he tried to roll over on one side, perhaps obeying an instinct to recover it, but he could not do it. Strange husky sounds were coming from him and he began coughing and a gout of blood burst from his mouth and he fell back and lay still.

When Fallon looked up, gunsmoke still drifting about him, the acrid smell of burnt powder in his nostrils, he saw Fran, ashen-faced, walking towards him. "Jody?"

"Jody's all right. He fell, winded himself. Ray LePage is hurt."

Emily had come out of the general store and saw her husband walking up from the other end of Main. Allott said to Fallon, as he drew nearer: "Sheriff Stoll is up at the barbershop, badly shot."

"Will he live?"

Allott sighed. "Mitchell says that if he survives another twelve hours or so, he will. Mitchell's done all he can."

Fallon walked across and looked down at Crane, Fran with him. "He came here by chance," he said. "Maybe he'll be the only one."

She did not answer him. "Come on," he said. "I want to talk with Jody."

★ ★ ★

The morning was blazing hot. Sleeman, though still quiet with shock, was beginning to move once more. The doctor from the town of Kendall, some forty miles north, was preparing to climb into his covered buggy.

"Too damn' hot for this," he said, "but there's no choice. I've got patients to see to." He looked one last time at Mitchell in the doorway of his barbershop. "When your sheriff is back on his feet the first thing he ought to do is shake you by the hand. By rights he should be in his grave." He nodded, flicked the reins and moved away, trailing dust.

Near the other end of Main, LePage, stogie between his teeth, stood somewhat stiffly outside his saloon, for under his fancy shirt and waistcoat he was firmly bandaged.

"You should still be in your bed," Allie told him. When he simply smiled, she said: "For a man who preached about not taking any risks and told all and sundry on no account to go out on the street, you've got gall to stand there grinning." With a whip of skirts she turned and went inside, leaving the batwings wagging.

Further down the street went Jody Fallon with a gaggle of chattering children. LePage raised a hand briefly to the boy's father, the tall man in the white apron, brooming the boardwalk outside the general store, then he too turned and followed Allie into The Black Horse.

Fran came out. Both of them stepped back for a better look at the bold new sign that had been painted on the board: JAMES FALLON, GENERAL STORE.

"Come what may, come who may," Fallon had said, "that's who I am, and this is where we live."

Fran went in, leaving Fallon to his sweeping, but not long afterwards he heard a noise, and her clear voice called to him: "Jim! Freight's here!"

## Other titles in the Linford Western Library:

### TOP HAND
#### Wade Everett

The Broken T was big. But no ranch is big enough to let a man hide from himself.

### GUN WOLVES OF LOBO BASIN
#### Lee Floren

The Feud was a blood debt. When Smoke Talbot found the outlaws who gunned down his folks he aimed to nail their hide to the barn door.

### SHOTGUN SHARKEY
#### Marshall Grover

The westbound coach carrying the indomitable Larry and Stretch headed for a shooting showdown.

## FIGHTING RAMROD
### Charles N. Heckelmann

Most men would have cut their losses, but Frazer counted the bullets in his guns and said he'd soak the range in blood before he'd give up another inch of what was his.

## LONE GUN
### Eric Allen

Smoke Blackbird had been away too long. The Lequires had seized the Blackbird farm, forcing the Indians and settlers off, and no one seemed willing to fight! He had to fight alone.

## THE THIRD RIDER
### Barry Cord

Mel Rawlins wasn't going to let anything stand in his way. His father was murdered, his two brothers gone. Now Mel rode for vengeance.

## ARIZONA DRIFTERS
### W. C. Tuttle

When drifting Dutton and Lonnie Steelman decide to become partners they find that they have a common enemy in the formidable Thurston brothers.

## TOMBSTONE
### Matt Braun

Wells Fargo paid Luke Starbuck to outgun the silver-thieving stagecoach gang at Tombstone. Before long Luke can see the only thing bearing fruit in this eldorado will be the gallows tree.

## HIGH BORDER RIDERS
### Lee Floren

Buckshot McKee and Tortilla Joe cut the trail of a border tough who was running Mexican beef into Texas. They stopped the smuggler in his tracks.

## BRETT RANDALL, GAMBLER
### E. B. Mann

Larry Day had the choice of running away from the law or of assuming a dead man's place. No matter what he decided he was bound to end up dead.

## THE GUNSHARP
### William R. Cox

The Eggerleys weren't very smart. They trained their sights on Will Carney and Arizona's biggest blood bath began.

## THE DEPUTY OF SAN RIANO
### Lawrence A. Keating and
### Al. P. Nelson

When a man fell dead from his horse, Ed Grant was spotted riding away from the scene. The deputy sheriff rode out after him and came up against everything from gunfire to dynamite.

## FARGO: MASSACRE RIVER
### John Benteen

The ambushers up ahead had now blocked the road. Fargo's convoy was a jumble, a perfect target for the insurgents' weapons!

## SUNDANCE: DEATH IN THE LAVA
### John Benteen

The Modoc's captured the wagon train and its cargo of gold. But now the halfbreed they called Sundance was going after it . . .

## HARSH RECKONING
### Phil Ketchum

Five years of keeping himself alive in a brutal prison had made Brand tough and careless about who he gunned down . . .

# FARGO: PANAMA GOLD
## John Benteen

With foreign money behind him, Buckner was going to destroy the Panama Canal before it could be completed. Fargo's job was to stop Buckner.

# FARGO: THE SHARPSHOOTERS
## John Benteen

The Canfield clan, thirty strong were raising hell in Texas. Fargo was tough enough to hold his own against the whole clan.

# PISTOL LAW
## Paul Evan Lehman

Lance Jones came back to Mustang for just one thing — revenge! Revenge on the people who had him thrown in jail.

## HELL RIDERS
### Steve Mensing

Wade Walker's kid brother, Duane, was locked up in the Silver City jail facing a rope at dawn. Wade was a ruthless outlaw, but he was smart, and he had vowed to have his brother out of jail before morning!

## DESERT OF THE DAMNED
### Nelson Nye

The law was after him for the murder of a marshal — a murder he didn't commit. Breen was after him for revenge — and Breen wouldn't stop at anything . . . blackmail, a frameup . . . or murder.

## DAY OF THE COMANCHEROS
### Steven C. Lawrence

Their very name struck terror into men's hearts — the Comancheros, a savage army of cutthroats who swept across Texas, leaving behind a bloodstained trail of robbery and murder.

# SUNDANCE: SILENT ENEMY
## John Benteen

... was on a ... needed to ... crazed ... undance.

# LASSITER
## Jack Slade

Lassiter wasn't the kind of man to listen to reason. Cross him once and he'll hold a grudge for years to come — if he let you live that long.

# LAST STAGE TO GOMORRAH
## Barry Cord

Jeff Carter, tough ex-riverboat gambler, now had himself a horse ranch that kept him free from gunfights and card games. Until Sturvesant of Wells Fargo showed up.